Chronicle of an Hour and a Half

SAHARU NUSAIBA KANNANARI

cntxt

First published by Context, an imprint of Westland Publications Private Limited, in 2024

No. 269/2B, First Floor, 'Irai Arul', Vimalraj Street, Nethaji Nagar, Alapakkam Main Road, Maduravoyal, Chennai 600095

Westland, the Westland logo, Context and the Context logo are the trademarks of Nasadiya Technologies Private Limited, or its affiliates.

ISBN: 9789360458096

10 9 8 7 6 5 4 3 2 1

This is a work of fiction. Names, characters, organisations, places, events and incidents are either products of the author's imagination or used fictitiously.

Typeset by SÜRYA, New Delhi

Printed at Manipal Technologies Limited, Manipal

To

V.P. Nusaiba Beevi

My first teacher. Beloved mother.

'I could just remember how my father used to say that the reason for living was to get ready to stay dead a long time.'

– William Faulkner, *As I Lay Dying*

'The future belongs to crowds.'

– Don Delillo, *Mao II*

Nabeesumma

He gave me five children and then he rested, like God after Creation.

He gave me five sons even before the fifth anniversary of our marriage. He named them Ibrahim, Imran, Dulqar, Rashid and Burhan. Then he rested while I eked out a living scrubbing dishes, washing clothes, mopping floors, tailoring churidars and salwars and blouses, dialling numbers all day at a telephone booth, rolling beedis for a local cooperative brand, sewing and stuffing mattresses and pillows with kapok fibre for the Communist Mattress Company.

All this while I wiped my children's bottoms, suckled them to ruddy health until my breasts were flat, took their clothes to the stream in the predawn dark and thrashed them clean, let out all the chickens and ducks from the coops in the morning and coaxed them back in at dusk, swept the yard strewn with teak and jackfruit and mahogany leaves, quarrelled with all the aluminium pots and pans in the kitchen, broke damp coconut husks and damp wood with machete and hatchet and pushed them into the sawdust stove and lit the fire by blowing through a pipe as long as my arm, cooked and fed the boys chickpea and yam and horse gram and beef and fish and partridge so that they grew as big as their father. All this while he lay by my side, snoring and farting, or lounged in his wicker chair reading the obituary column in the third newspaper expecting his fifth black tea before breakfast, or else followed me around the house nagging me about his piles, his chronic constipation. Sometimes I can't believe he gave me five children, that I brought up five sons who grew just as big and useless as their father, that at forty-nine I still have to eke out a living to feed all the jobless men in the house. In this leaking house.

When they came I was alone in the house, counting the leaking holes in the roof and, believe me, there were thirty. Thirty. It's a wonder the house has not yet collapsed. But then it's also a wonder Nabeesu has not collapsed either, or gone mad. Even this morning I asked my husband if he had any intention of repairing the roof, or throwing a tarp over it at least. But he said nothing. He just stood there looking at me with that look he had when he had finally given up on impregnating me, realising he couldn't do it any more. Sure, I understood, and then I had gone and stood by the kitchen door, looking out at the dark rainy morning, scribbling on my mind thoughts without language. At noon it was raining harder and darker when they came.

Reyhana

My husband gave me everything, including his kidney. He built me a house on a small hill that looked over the paddy fields and the stream and the road that ran right between them towards the Bazaar. A two-storey house from where in the mornings and evenings I could watch happy children in their colourful uniforms rush to school and return home. From where I could watch the progress of Burhan's flashlight as he approached my house at night like a secret.

It's the strangest feeling. This curious fate of having to carry inside me a vital organ of a man I hate to call mine. Is there a stranger bondage? It has none of the comforts of an unknown donor. A hockey-stick scar etched into the right of my abdomen. Its pain is to conscience what phantom pain is to limb. Injecting a sense of indebtedness into an otherwise endlessly dragging drama of apartness. It's the guiltiest feeling, too. Capable of incarcerating you in the very place you don't belong. But I couldn't have refused, could I? Our small-town doctors discovered what I was dying from too late as usual, after the routine half-a-dozen misdiagnoses and months of mistreatment, and there wasn't much time to think and wait. Besides, I was too young to die.

I was too young to die.

If someone were to commit my life to words, they would have to spend page after boring page on my kidney predicaments. This, the existence of a foreign kidney inside my body, purifying my blood, was the only philosophical question in my life. Did I want to die? No. Did he want me to die? No. Did I want his kidney? I was conflicted, I would say. My conscience sparred and ached, but I had no choice. Did he want me to have his kidney? Yes. Yes. Yes. One of my cousins with the same blood group and matching kidney was ready to donate hers, but Sadique wouldn't let her. I suspect he even blocked a possible donor and bribed the doctor to make sure that I lived the rest of my life on his kidney, not on someone else's, in debt forever. And it turned out to be a miraculous kidney, too.

The body knows nothing about the mind and its hundred predicaments. The doctors counselled me through the possibility that my body might reject the organ and the disease might recur. The frankest among them even gave me a trial period of six to sixteen months, promised me ten more years of life in case of a success, pointed out the inevitability of years of continuous medication and dietary regulations even if things went fine. And then they sent me to sleep. When I woke up, I was on his kidney. My life had changed and I felt like a foreigner in my own body. My miserable life was made hellish by that single haunting knowledge. It made liquid the very air I breathed. But my mental agony had no bearing on my physical health because my body didn't reject his kidney even though it had more than enough reasons to do so and I ate anti-rejection capsules and blood pressure stabilisers and my physical health improved steadily and, three years after the transplantation, I was three years younger again, astonishing the doctors. But the improvement in my physical health in no way corresponded to my mental health and my mental health declined. Steadily. Eroding even the remotest consolations of this unfortunate matrimony.

To allow yourself to marry a man you don't like: that's the wrongest morality. To not have the will to break free from its bondage is a sister shame.

Lack of love in itself is not an unendurable burden. No, I don't think so. Not that it's unimportant, but one could live with lack of love, or learn to. I would have been just fine if my husband was just boring and innocuous like Doordarshan. But he was a suffocating presence, an unsettling shadow that hovered at the back of my mind even through deep sleep.

I was tired living his life and I had to violate it in some way.

When you are immured in an unhappy marriage, crippled by your own immense lack of will to break free, what better half-consolation than an unemotional, irresponsible, liberating affair? I wanted to do it at thirty and I began doing it finally at forty, exactly two months ago, when I sweated it out with Burhan, in a bed that reeked of my sleepless years, and each night was like a private revenge on Sadique C.T., my husband.

What was I revenging? Just unhappiness? I can't tell you more than that. I can't tell you what exactly I loathed about him aside from his dark skin and his brushy moustache and his weepy dependence. But resentment towards him has long been absorbed in me as smoke is by lungs. It clings to me like a tenacious layer of mud I can't wipe off. And yet I can't tell you what I hated in him so much. After all, my husband did give me everything. He gave me not only a beautiful house and a great kidney but also two daughters, twins who looked so much alike that the sight bewildered me when I first laid eyes on them after I had pushed them out of my womb, twenty-three years ago.

They live and study together, the twins. Always together. Dressing up alike and confounding everyone. They live in a hostel run by nuns in Thrissur, where they are students at the Government Medical College. 'Do you miss them?' I remember Burhan asking me once, his otherwise restless eyes still for once in sincere curiosity, plunging my mind momentarily into a crisis that was at once familiar and answerless. 'Yes, I do,' I had said, wondering if I really did, knowing how strongly the twins reminded me of their father, adding confusedly, 'but not so much,' because, after all, it was in their absence that I had Burhan for a man. I remember evading his eyes and resting my head on his warm hairy chest in thoughtless happiness because, believe me, even in our most sentimental embrace, he was freedom. A lover most unlike Sadique, that uxorious leech.

Sadique always wanted to talk on the phone and he wanted to talk for long hours. That was his way of fighting his sexless expatriate solitude. He would call me from his flat in suburban Riyadh before breakfast and during lunch and after dinner and whenever he was free from work, eternally irritating. Even today I was talking to him when Burhan texted me at noon. Burhan texted that he was at the mosque, that he planned to come over once congregation dispersed. He didn't ask me if he could but I wouldn't have refused anyway—I couldn't have.

Yes, I texted back.

Imam Shahnavaz

It was time to wind up today's topic: God's omnipresence. I studied the bored congregants. 'God is in everything and God is everywhere,' I said. 'In everything alive and in everything dead. Without death. Like plastic.' They all looked up from the floor of the mosque. Their faces were sleepy and slack, like attendees of some common dream too immediate to disentangle from, too fleeting to ponder over.

Among them I noticed Burhan, Nabeesumma's youngest. He was busy on his phone. 'He is even in the mike I speak into. He is even in your phone,' I said. A few of the congregants looked at each other in silent confusion and then they turned their eyes towards the rain. So I too turned my eyes and watched the rain, mighty and roaring. It made me wonder how long the electricity would last. I turned my gaze back to the hall of sleepers. I studied them row by row. Burhan was sitting in the fifth row, near the pulpit, and he was busy on his phone still, unstirred by my admonition.

Nothing agitates me as Imam more than a congregant busy on his phone during the Friday sermon. Nothing violates the sanctity of the mosque more than a congregant busy on his phone during the Friday sermon. Nothing. Not even sleep. I fixed my eyes on Burhan and said, 'God is Made in China. He is in everything and he is everywhere. He is even in your phone. To doubt him, to mock him, to refute him is as useless and punishable as Marxism at 2 a.m.'

Burhan put his phone in his shirt pocket and turned his head left. I turned with him and saw the rain again, dark and deafening. It made me worry about the clay tiles and the rotten rafters. I looked up at the gable where pigeons had found refuge, wet and crooning and pecking under their wings, their dirty feathers coming down in a slow breezy negotiation of gravity. I looked down at the congregants and they were all watching the rain, as hypnotised as before. I watched the rain, one among them for a long moment. It was raining for the sixth day without a let-up. Night after night you went to sleep with the rain and in the morning, even before you woke up, even before you opened your mind's eyes before opening your actual eyes, your ears heard the rain. I heard an owl hoot and the pigeons panicked in a din of wings. I looked up at the gable and saw the owl spread its wings, I saw its long legs and their socks of plumage, their dirty feathers sinking in the air, whirling like leaves that smelt of rain. Rain and darkness.

I declared the sermon over and stepped down from the pulpit. A sibilant murmur of relief spread among the congregants as they rose from the floor. The muezzin put his fingers in his ears and called for prayer. A hush descended over the hall.

Ashraf

As soon as the prayers ended, everyone jumped up and rushed to the door and stood watching the madness of the rain. Brown water ran like undammed streams down the slope towards the road. The porch was crowded. Everyone was eager to go home but we were all trapped by the sheer intensity of the deluge, which we gawked at, huddled together like wet chickens. Beside me were Burhan, Shahid and the Imam. The Imam whispered to Burhan, phone something.

'This is the darkest monsoon,' I said, interrupting the Imam.

'They always say that here,' Burhan said.

'What do they say here?' I said.

'That it's the darkest monsoon. That's what they always say here every year.' Then he threw his large four-fold umbrella open and lurched hurriedly out into the rain and vanished in the watery blindness.

The Imam turned to Shahid and said, 'Not since 1991.'

Shahid said, 'I can't tell because I was only a kid in knickers in 1991,' and laughed. The Imam stared at him and he stopped laughing. The Imam continued to stare at him even though he wasn't laughing any more. Nobody said anything more for a couple of minutes and we continued to watch the rain in silence until the Imam said, 'Shahid, let's go. It's no good waiting.' And, with a sigh, 'Not since 1991.'

They opened their umbrellas and stepped out into the rain. Somebody patted my shoulder and I turned. It was Imran, Burhan's brother. He was standing where the Imam had been standing a moment ago, right beside me, with a queer smile on his lips.

'You don't have an umbrella like your brother to go home?' I said.

'Mine is with Burhan.'

'And where is his?'

'He hasn't got one.'

'And he is gone,' I said. 'I saw him a few minutes ago. He left right after Hakimaakka.'

'That's okay. I can get under Ibrahim's.'

'And where is he?'

'Must be somewhere around. Inside the mosque maybe.'

We watched the rain. The Imam was right, I thought. The weather was in fact eerily reminiscent of 1991. I was fifteen at the time and I have a clear memory of it. All the schools were closed and towns were deserted—life had come to a standstill. Snakes were everywhere, cattle were turning up dead, their bellies distended and on the verge of explosion. The news of landslides kept coming from the upper hills and everyone anxiously tuned their radios to government advisories and the latest updates from the meteorological department. Trees were uprooted and roads were washed away and bridges were ripped asunder. Wells were overflowing and crops were laid waste. The days were dark as night and sleep was febrile and the sun was the single protagonist in everyone's dream.

I said to Imran, 'It's all going back to 1991.' But he said nothing, just shook his chin in agreement and disbelief.

The stormy turn of the weather surprised us all. We had not seen it coming. It had been raining for six days, but the trees were dead-still and there was no wind to speak of. But now the windows and the doors of the mosque banged from wall to wall in violent repetitions. *Dhaak dhaak dhaak.* Someone howled *hoooo.* The storm chased some people from the porch back into the mosque. Umbrellas were opening. Spokes were breaking. I folded my mundu and tied it tightly round my waist and stood still watching the circus of the wind. Lightning blazed across the sky in a great bluish fury and thunder crashed with Quranic wrath and then it was all dark again. I thought of Pathumma and June, my wife and daughter. I opened my umbrella and started for home.

Ahmad

When the wind began raging I rushed back inside the mosque. It's a big hall divided by a green curtain right in the middle and I could hear the women chattering on the other side. I rolled up a plastic mat for headrest and lay down on the floor. I decided not to head home because there were no dry clothes in the almirah and if I were to reach home soaked in the rain, Nabeesu would soap and thrash what I wore as well to revenge her lifelong suffering so that I would have no clean clothes to go out in any more. She was capable of such small acts of revenge. She could deny me the luxury of clean dry underwear on a merry Bakrid morning. She bore a tumorous hate for me, a humongous one, perpetually growing since our marriage, which may go on growing even long after I am dead and gone for all I know. She has said that to me in no uncertain terms, that I was such a burden that even my death cannot unburden her. It's not often you get a wife as outspoken as Nabeesu around here. But it's also true that you don't get a wife as hardworking as Nabeesu around here. At sixty-three I look a lot younger than her. There are times when I regret not being helpful to her, not having had a job, especially when I see my own children, who all turned out to be just as useless as me. It's a legend in the village that Nabeesu has six children, not five. The legend is that I am her illegitimate sixth. I, Ahmad, her husband.

Nabeesu is two good feet shorter than all of us and yet she has a way of throwing her eyes into my eyes, point blank, blaming me for it all. It was the same look she had in her eyes this morning when she asked me if I intended to repair the roof or at least throw a tarp over the leaking house. She had been asking me that question for a good week before the monsoon had arrived with a deafening clamour in the dark middle of the humid night.

Point blank. Blaming me for it all: the five useless sons, the mice, the crumbling house with thirty dripping holes in the roof like thirty metaphors for the years she had been married to me.

I lay down on the floor of the mosque thinking about tarp, the money for it.

A full repair was out of the question, which, aside from being expensive, would have required us to open up the entire roof and replace the rotten rafters and the broken tiles and I couldn't have stood the noise of it all, the sheer labour of it all. So I let the summer pass because I couldn't bear to hear the *greeng greeng greeng* of the saw or the *dhaak dhaak dhaak* of the hammer for a whole day as carpenter Ismael and his underpaid apprentices drove nails in each joint afresh or sawed the rafters to size. So I let the monsoon come because no carpenter climbs on to the roof and does roof-carpentry in the rain, not even Ismael. It was to be the tarp then, and I have been thinking of tarp ever since it began raining, thinking about the money for it. For a while I entertained the idea that Nabeesu would give up and give me the money as usual but, after six days of rain, I had abandoned that hope.

I am sure she had nagged each of her five useless beards separately, asking for money, and I am sure none of them had said yes to her nagging, her beseeching. You couldn't nag money out of them, partly because they do nothing for a stable earning and partly because they are all selfish, numb to her grey misery. They all have the money for each of their needs, to buy shoes and shirts and jeans and phones, to buy 150cc motorcycles with loans from Tamil usurers even without a nameable job. What they don't have the money for is the household, towards meeting the bills and providing for food and a little bit for their parents' daily expenses. But Nabeesu would have tried all the same, knowing none of them would pay her for the tarp, because most of the holes in the roof were towards the kitchen and the dining room and they didn't have much business there. I tend to think that if the leaks were on their side of the roof, one of them would have paid, but the leaks were confined to the dining room and the kitchen and they couldn't have cared less. For that Nabeesu would have to sew churidars at home or mattresses at her communist company. Because that's how she has been feeding her six children all these years.

I have been unusually bothered by all this of late. So, this morning, as each of them unbolted their doors, I had a tremendous itch to ask my sons to pay a little bit for the household expenses but I didn't. I didn't partly because I have been such a sloth all my life and unkind to Nabeesu in every respect and partly because they were all quarrelsome, my sons, at the slightest spark their temper would soar up in flames, and Nabeesu would have been upset if her husband and sons were to pick a quarrel and shout at each other on a holy Friday morning.

The way it was raining reminded me of 1991, terrible old 1991. Water wouldn't cease rising and hills were sliding like sand and trees were crashing.

1991 was terrible. Nabeesu was pregnant one last time with Burhan and the roof had collapsed. 1991 was the last and only time we ever replaced the rafters. 1991 was terrible for the other reason too. How can I forget? It was the year impotency undid me, depriving me of the last and only source of pleasure in my life.

I have always been lazy, even before marriage. I was an only son and my parents were conveniently dead. For a while I shepherded my mother's goats, but by the time I was twenty-five,

I had sold them as well. I ate at my aunt's two times a day and did nothing. At my aunt's everyone ridiculed me. Seven-foot-nothing, they called me in audible whispers even though I was only six-foot-two. It seemed to me that my height had made my slothfulness particularly unattractive, that if I were a little shorter, they would have despised me a little less.

So they found for me a woman. One day they decided that I was too tall to be taken care of like a barren cow, too bearded, too old. It was their secret ploy to deny me my two meals a day, and before I could fully comprehend what was happening, marriage happened. I was thirty-three or thirty-four then. One day my uncle and cousins invited me for a formal feast at my aunt's and informed me that my informal meals were over. I had to feed two now and I didn't know how. After the marriage, Nabeesu waited for me to say something and she waited for weeks, silent and distant. She continued her silence even as I began unhooking her little gold necklaces, and then, one after the other, her bracelets and anklets and even her silver ring disappeared into the bank coffers until the only metal left to hock on her body was the golden aranjnanam that hung idly on her hips. It was when I began to unhook her aranjnanam from behind that I experienced for the first time that point-blank look—challenging and threatening and unrelenting and unforgettable. I stopped unhooking right away, but she unhooked the aranjnanam herself and said, 'Go buy me a sewing machine.'

A full repair was what was needed, I knew, but I had let the summer pass and let the monsoon fall, and now it was to be the tarp, far less expensive. I thought about the money for it. And, as usual, it all came down to Nabeesu. I made up my mind to steal from her secret stash of cash hidden in the rice vessel and to blame it on the children, like I had done twice before. It had worked.

All the doors to the mosque were closed, all but the front one. The front door was crowded. Everyone was stranded. Trapped. The storm had puzzled everyone, even me, and I have not been interested in anything except the weather for much of my life, and I could tell it was going to be worse than 1991. That is, if it was going to continue raining like this for another week. I could hear the men on the porch, the boys milling about. I could hear devotees all around me, young and old, reciting the Quran, in groups or alone in the darkened hall. Women susurrating behind the curtain and children disporting and the Quran-reciters crying *hush hush hush.* And I lay among them, thinking my tarp thoughts, my Nabeesu thoughts, even as I fell asleep, hearing them all, hearing my own snoring.

Pathumma

I told my child not to combine fish and milk. It's not healthy, I said. 'If you eat fish and drink milk together you'll have vitiligo and then you'll be no different from one of those piebald horses on your Animal Planet. And then no handsome man will marry you.'

She continued eating fish and drinking milk, watching Animal Planet. She never listens to me, my child. She has always loved her father Ashraf just a little more. June is our only child, our tantrum girl, twelve years old. I went to the kitchen and watched the torrential downpour. My thoughts went back to that time when my father sat me on his shoulders and walked with my mother down the hill after a couple of landslides had torn the upper hills in tremendous explosions. I remembered how in the deep grey of that old dawn, my legs wound around my father's neck, his hands holding my ankles tight, drenched like sponge, shivering in the rain, we plodded down the hill without umbrellas, leaving the house behind forever. I remembered that time. I remembered without wanting to. I remembered because of the rain.

My child said she was missing her antlions.

I turned around. She was standing by the door, looking at me. 'Juuune,' I cried. 'Stop being a baby. You are a twelve-year-old, not a five-year-old. Antlions will skid backwards down into the centre of their little whirls of dust come next summer.' She said she couldn't wait until the next summer and I said even I couldn't imagine the next summer or expect to see the sun or the moon anytime soon, with the rain falling like pellets for the sixth day, each day getting darker than the one before and the nights colder and noisier. She went back to her chair in the dining room. I walked out to the porch and looked out. It was too dark to see. Vague and ghostly, I could see four men dressed in white emerge from the dark shroud of the rain, in single file, like figures on film or the djinns I used to imagine as a child. I could see their umbrellas, long-handled and long-ferruled, their large black canopies keeping them slow and a little distant from each other. They approached my house and stopped outside the porch, knee-deep in the water

The oldest of them said, 'Which one is Burhan's house?'

I pointed towards Nabeesumma's house saying, 'That one.'

They said nothing more. They went back and walked along

the trail towards Nabeesumma's house, one of them their father, I assumed, and the other three his children, fair and tall and bearded and strong as their father. A wind grew and the trees along the trail rocked and the leaves blew tensely in a stormy presentiment. I waited for the wind and thunder and I didn't have to wait for long. My child began to yell from the dining room, in response I thought. I stomped back into the house. But no, her yelling had nothing to do with the dramatic change in the weather. She said she wanted more fish and milk. 'No,' I said. 'Go and cry.'

June

I heard the thunder. But it was a small thunder and I was not distracted. I continued watching TV, waiting for Ippa. I was watching TV, eating fish and drinking milk. Imma was angry. Talking to herself. Fish and milk. I wanted more but Imma said No. The power went off and I yelled in the dark for more fish and milk. The power came back on and on the table was a plate full of anchovies and a glass full of cow milk and I stopped yelling. I changed the channels and watched animal things. I wasn't watching TV because I wanted to watch TV. I was watching TV to watch the screen as the power went off. When the power went off, the TV would go off with a sucking sound, leaving a green circle in the middle of the screen. It all happened quickly, true, but I liked watching it.

I kept changing channels, watching animal things. Eating

fish and drinking milk. Waiting for Ippa. Then first the doors slammed and then the windows banged and then I heard the trees. I felt the thunder before I heard it. I felt the thunder right under my feet before I screamed and I heard the thunder only after I started screaming. And then I saw. I saw the blue light of lightning before the power went off. I saw the blue light before I opened my eyes. And I was screaming. Then I heard the door open again. I opened my eyes and looked. Imma was holding the door, looking out. Imma closed the door. I could still hear the trees. I could still feel the thunder. I could still see the lightning, its blue shock. The rain kept falling. Like yesterday. Like the day before yesterday. And the day before that. I saw the lightning but there was no sucking sound or a green circle on the TV when the power went off this time. I could see the light of the match before I heard Imma strike the match. She placed a wax candle on the table, right next to me. Its flame was blue. Steady and blue.

We didn't talk, Imma and I. For a moment I looked at her but she wasn't looking at me. She was looking at the flame. Steady and blue. Hearing the rain. Hearing the trees. It thundered right beneath my feet, touched my feet before I heard it. Then came the blue shock. I saw its violence in the plugholes, crackling and sparkling. I could hear fuses blowing up somewhere in the house. I could smell the smoke. Through the windows I saw the mahogany trees and their wet leaves. Like in X-ray sheets. In the clearest blue. And I screamed *Ippaaa.* Imma came with a wax candle. She lit the candle with a match, held it upside down until it dripped three fat drops on to the table, and then stuck it firmly on them. And the candle stuck. It began to flicker a little now. The flame. In soft sweet blue. Like kerosene. We sat face-to-face without looking at each other. Waiting for Ippa. For sure Ippa would ask Imma why the candle was on the dining table, why not on a piece of paper, why not on the bottom of a steel plate. I thought of warning Imma that Ippa was going to ask about the candle when he came but I didn't. Instead, I tried to imagine the antlions, but I couldn't imagine summer. I took three anchovies from the plate and began to eat them one by one, watching Imma, but Imma wasn't watching me. She was looking beyond my shoulder. I could hear the crunch of the anchovies between my teeth. I could taste the oozing coconut oil in my mouth.

The flame was longer now, blue flame with bluer crest. It was one o'clock but around us the darkness was total. Like yesterday. Like the day before yesterday. And the day before that. Ever since the rain began. Six nights ago, around midnight. And then it was raining, from morning to morning. The chickens and ducks were numb in their coops, sleeping and sleeping and waking only to peek and peck at their bowls of wet rice, to chase lice from under their damp wings, and cats were under the stacks of wood in the backyard which Ippa had covered with a blue plastic sheet, starving and meowing maybe, but I couldn't have heard because of the rain. All the squirrels and all the birds were gone. Even the crows were gone. On the walls the spiders had stopped moving. The lizards were still. Like dead long ago. Day and night we watched the roof, the rafters for snakes. The floors were damp. Smelt like my damp clothes. Our feet left prints on the black floor. The dining room smelt of dead flying termites from the previous days. But yesterday there were no flying termites. Nor today. Imma had the candle flame in her blue eyes. Her eyes were bluer than the candle's blue flame, flickering in the centre of her eyes. Imma's eyes weren't blinking. Imma never blinked. I looked at Imma's eyes but Imma was looking at the candle flame getting bluer and bluer all the time but not bluer than Imma's eyes which were bluer than blue. Imma's chin was in the pit of her palm. Imma was expecting Ippa to forget his umbrella so she could blame him before he could blame her for anything at all. Ippa forgot his umbrella all the time. He often came home wet in the rain saying he had forgotten it again.

Then the door opened.

We both turned and looked. The umbrella was wet but Ippa was wetter. I could hear the rain and the wind. Ippa shut the door behind him. He was drenched.

'Ain, Moley,' he said.

They named me Ainmatar. But everyone called me June because Imma called me June. Everyone except Ippa. Imma told me that they even had a quarrel over it. Imma loved the rain and she wanted to name me Mazha or June. Ippa didn't like either name because Ippa hated June and hated rain in general. But Imma said, Even my calendar starts with June, not January. Ippa said June sounded Christian and rejected June. And Ippa hated rain, so Mazha was out of the question. Besides, Mazha wasn't even Arabi. Imma said she and Ippa didn't talk for two days. A compromise had to be reached. Half a dozen years they had waited for me and how could all the happiness be squandered away like that, in silly squabbles over the name of the baby, Imma said. A compromise had to be reached. She accepted the Arabi part. The name should be Arabi, a Muslim without an Arabi name was like August without landslides, she said to Ippa. Find the equivalent of rain in Arabi. But name her Rain. And she would be called June. But Ippa hated the rain. A compromise had to be reached. So he named me Ainmatar. And Imma called me June. One official and one unofficial. One Muslim and one non-Muslim. Imma called me June. So everyone else also called me June. Everyone except Ippa. Ippa told me 'ain' meant eye in Arabi and 'matar' meant rain and that he would call me Ain. But if anybody else called me Ain, I wouldn't know they were calling me. Ippa called me Ain and I liked it better than June because, like Ippa, I hated the rain. I even ate with a spoon because otherwise I would have to wash my hands and I hated getting my hands wet. I hated water in general. I liked Ain more than Matar and June and far more than Mazha, so I liked Ippa more than Imma. So, the first thing I wanted to do when he opened the door and called me Ain was to rush towards him, but I didn't move because I saw he was wet and I didn't want to get wet.

I buried my feet under my skirt and just looked on. Ippa looked confused, as if he had forgotten something. As if only his body was here and his mind was elsewhere. The candle flame flickered violently and then died. I could see the light of the match before I heard Imma strike the match. Imma had an anchovy between her teeth. The flame of the candle was less blue. Less steady. Unsure. As if it knew Ippa was going to pull the door open again. Imma cupped the flame with her palms. Imma's hands glowed pink with fire. The flame was now even less blue, unsteady. With a pinch of gold and a tinge of pink and grains of grainy green. The flame died even before Ippa pulled the door open. I could hear the trees. I could feel the tiny pain of the thousand specks of glass the rain was sprinkling on my bare arms and legs. The wind was in the trees and I could hear the trees. I could smell the light. I could hear the rain. Falling. Falling. Falling.

'Can you hear the trees, Imma?' I said. 'You heard a tree fall, Imma?'

Imma didn't answer. It was colder in the dark. My T-shirt was sleeveless and my hands were wedged in my armpits. I waited for Imma to strike the match and light the candle, hating the rain, waiting to be called June and hating June, but Imma did neither. We had been waiting for Ippa, and then Ippa came in and went out and we were now waiting again. We were waiting for Ippa because we wanted to have lunch and Imma never had her lunch without Ippa. Imma never let me eat my lunch without Ippa. Certainly not on Fridays. I ate my fish and drank my milk because I had to keep eating and Imma couldn't complain because, no matter how much I ate, I never grew fat.

Hakimaakka

I was the first one to leave the mosque and I reached home around the time the weather took a turn for the worse. I changed my clothes and dragged a chair to the kitchen and sat with Ramlath, my wife, watching the rain. I smoked my cigarette and thought of my father. He died a week ago but I could still hear his dry coughs. He was dying of cancer anyway but he chose to die of a silent heart attack. I saw my father dying. He walked towards the sofa and lay down and closed his eyes for a nap from which he never awoke. So maybe I can't say I saw him die because I only saw him fall asleep. I could only see him sleeping, not coughing his dry waterless cough any more, just lying there, eyes closed and asleep, sound asleep. He died a week ago and that was the last day we saw the sun. I smoked my cigarette and thought of my dead father, still hearing his coughs.

My phone rang and Ramlath told me not to connect the call because of the lightning. It was ringing from under the gas stove and I asked her to lean over a bit and get it for me. She gave me the phone saying, 'Molu.' Our eldest daughter. I said, 'Hello Molu, *aa, enthaadee*?' Molu told me to pass the phone to her mother. I did, but she pushed the phone back to me saying, Lightning lightning. So I said to Molu, Look, your mother is going to tell me whatever you are going to tell her as soon as the call is over. Lightning flashed and lashed, leaving the rain glittering in its wake. Cut the call, Ramlath cried.

Molu said she was two months down. I thought of clearing my throat but I didn't.

'Well,' I said. 'You say another cub is on the way. That's good news. Congratulations.'

Molu said she was tired of pregnancies.

'Well,' I said, 'that's good news too.'

Then Molu began to weep. I listened as her mother looked on with a gaze that understood everything. She always understood everything without being told, or at least had a certain look that said she understood everything. She had a knack for that. A knack for looking like she understood. And she understood, mostly. This piece of information she certainly did. Molu went on weeping. This was her fourth. Her husband was on an eternal hunt for a boy. Her husband was Mr District and dumbbell dumb. Muscles everywhere but hollow in the head. He simply couldn't accept the fact that he was unable to father a son in the first three attempts despite all the muscles. He didn't understand that a father's muscles are not a deciding factor in the sex of the baby. Molu went on weeping and I waited for her to hush. A toad landed on my ankle and then leapt towards the wall. My first instinct was to chase it out but I didn't. Molu's weeping was hushing now.

'Would you hush now?' I said. She stopped weeping. 'Hush now and your mother will talk to you as soon as there's some let-up in the rain.'

I waited for her to disconnect the call but she didn't, so I disconnected the call and turned towards that all-understanding look of my wife, her mother. She snatched the phone away in anger and put it under the gas stove. She turned back to me, still furious. She said nothing, so I said nothing. All understanding.

It seemed to be raining harder. It seemed to be raining harder all the time. At the mosque people were talking about the swelling river and the flooding paddy fields and the football fields. Outside the grand door of the old mosque there was a hill of wet black umbrellas, like a pile of dead fruit bats. Inside the mosque the Imam was boring as usual. And, as usual, today also I fell asleep like everyone else in that ancient hall. I told Ramlath what the Imam spoke about in his sermon today. That God is like plastic. That God is Made in China. He is in everything. He is everywhere. She said nothing.

Water rushed down the backyard towards the trail below. On the trees the leaves had turned a dense green. On the kitchen walls there were rain snails and small white-capped monsoon mushrooms. The trunk of the great jackfruit tree was black and mossy green with dapples of magenta where the crust of the bark had peeled off. The great heavy jackfruit that hung from the middle of the trunk had cracked open in two, its yellow entrails rotting. The tapioca plants looked like they had been beheaded by the blowing wind that roared in the trees and Ramlath and I sat watching the ones we cared about in anxious premonition. Misfortunes have a way of seeking me out. Nine years ago, in October, in a shocking spree, lightning struck all six of my coconut trees dead—it was so bad we couldn't even cash the timber at any of the sawmills around town. It took them nine years to fruit and they were not older than fifteen when the divine electricity struck them dead. And four years ago, in June, one of my teaks landed on the kitchen—the walls and iron grills collapsed, the roof tiles and rafters crashed and cracked the floor open, and some of its branches were in the dining room, unpacking a thousand weaver ants from all their leafy mansions.

I drew my hand to my mouth to take a puff but my lips kissed cold fingers instead. The cigarette was gone. My memory of throwing it away was gone too.

A tree crashed and my heart stopped.

The mahogany crashed onto the cashew tree and for a moment I heard nothing else, saw nothing else, thought nothing else. For a moment I was numb. Then I sprang from my chair and went out into the mess to take stock of my loss.

I saw Ashraf coming up, hurrying across the trail towards my property. I waited for him.

'See the mess,' I shouted.

I stood looking at the trees, shivering in the rain. Ramlath was watching us, standing at the door of the kitchen. Misfortunes have a way of seeking me out. They strike exactly when I half-expect them. I wanted to say that to Ashraf but he wasn't looking at me. He wasn't looking at the trees. He was looking across the trail towards Nabeesumma's house. I followed his gaze. It was difficult to see in the pouring blindness, so we took few steps towards the trail. Nabeesumma was standing in the rain without an umbrella, talking to four men who weren't her husband or sons. The four men began to move again, in single file, with quick long strides, and she lurched after them, as though scared, almost begging. Then the men stopped because she overtook them and blocked their path. It was difficult to see because of the rain and the trees and all their large umbrellas. We only saw them blurrily. The men stopped abruptly because Nabeesumma had blocked their way, hands outstretched, like she was nailed to a cross, and then we saw her fall down to the ground. And they moved on. As though nothing had happened.

'Oh my God,' Ashraf said. 'Did you see that? The man just slapped Nabeesumma. Oh my.'

'Slap? What for?' I said. 'Why would anyone want to slap Nabeesumma?'

But he said nothing. We went down to help her but, by the time we reached the spot, she was already up on her feet, staring at us. She hurried back to her house before we could speak a word. We stood watching her, confused. But the rain and the wind were such that we couldn't have continued to stand where we were any longer. Ashraf asked me to follow him home. He set off and I followed, in wordless confusion.

Nabeesumma

Areacode, Areecode, Areakode, Areekode. Last week when I went to the Saturday Market with Burhan on his motorcycle to buy a couple of guinea chickens and some dried shark, there was a new spelling on a new kitchenware shop: Aricod. The small town on the banks of the Chaliyar River, where my home used to be until my parents married me off when I was nineteen years old.

They married me off across the river on a bright summer day in late May 1986. The water used to be much cleaner then and on a clear fourteenth night you could see the flawless dunes of white sands and little shadows of orange chromides and garfish and schools of giant danios as they swam, dimpling the surface in their trail. In deep summer the river used to shrink, baring the undulant sand dunes. As evening approached, they filled up with picnickers and sporters and hawkers. Kids ran with paper kites or traced iron fillings in the sands with bits of magnet wrapped in bits of paper. At dusk, just as the calls for maghrib prayers rose from all the mosques in and around the town and from the villages beyond the river, a thousand bats took flight from the dense palms along the banks in waves against the late colours of the sun. It was at this time of the year that the nomads with their obscure tongues and acrobatic children used to put up their canvas tents on the sands and set up their great circus and the nights were great fun. Then my parents married me off.

They came to my home on a boat, the groom and his aunties and uncles and the men from his village, and I went with them, down the stairs into the river, across the river on the same boat that brought them, and trekked four kilometres up the trails towards his home under the harsh blue sky and the white glaring sun through coconut hills, paddy and sesame fields, granite quarries, cashew orchards with their pungent red fruits, canopies of teaks with meandering trails flanked by wild pineapples redder than red roses and streams with boulders as old as the earth, with water clear as glass, infested with water spiders and trout still and pensive as hermits, black as rocks. Even then I was confused, walking with my groom who wore a white mundu and white polyester shirt with a plaited handkerchief tucked under its collar—fairer, older, a good two feet taller, yet somehow slower than me. Even then I was confused about this strange man, my life to come, the responsibility of having to give birth to children soon and the liability of having to love them more than myself because I was only nineteen and I wasn't finished loving myself enough.

I married him because he was fourteen years older than me and that single factor slashed the dowry by more than half and that was not a deal my father could have rejected even though my husband had no job. He got so late to marry because he was too lazy to marry. When my father asked him about his job, he said he would look for one with a kind of burdened assurance and my father agreed. He agreed because I had four younger sisters, waiting for their turn with all their burden of dowries and brown skin. And then I was pregnant each year, a ritual much like Ramzan, and each child was like a bomb, an explosion of confusion. I didn't even know that I had any part in it. The children were just coming out of me, despite myself, as if my body was growing new limbs without my own consent, and by the time I was aware, the house was full of their hungry noise, like a few eternally whistling pressure cookers, and I lay sleeplessly beside my husband who couldn't get it up in bed, not any more.

At first I refused to accept that I was their mother, that they were my children. I pretended that they were the children of a dead brother I never had. But they grow on you, children, and even though at first they were the limbs I never wanted, they soon became the limbs I couldn't cut off. And slowly I began to love them. Slowly, confusedly, with a kind of helpless indifference. I could feel the ache of Ibrahim's milk teeth on my nipples long after I had stopped suckling him and somehow I grew maternal without my own consent. In the quiet middle of the night I would be suckling two at a time while the other three went on crying and I felt like a helpless bitch with a limited number of udders and for a long time I didn't sleep. During the day I opened pods of kapok and stuffed mattresses with their fluffy fibre at the communist mattress company across the river and at night I pedalled the sewing machine *dreen dreen dreen* while the children clung like bats to my breasts and for a long time I didn't sleep. I don't remember when I finally fell asleep but, by the time I woke up, I had already become an old woman. My hair was grey, messy, tangled, as though, overnight, seasons had moved under my scalp in some dizzying spell, and in the mirror I looked like a mad harridan or a sorceress waking from some frightful trance. My knees were arthritic, my vision dim and hearing dull. Memories seemed to have fled and some kind of night had entered my eyes and mind and they were all no more than some dependent shadows. In my husband I saw my sons old and in my sons I saw my husband young. Each to the other synonymous—handsome, muscular, cranky, ungrateful. Useless.

Two weeks ago I went to my old mother across the river with a burlap sack full of husked coconuts to vent my frustration. I told her that my children were turning out to be just like my husband—useless.

'Lazy as kitchen cats. At this age they expect me to feed them,' I told her. 'I can't afford to even get sick.'

My mother said this was sad. 'Husbands,' she said, and sighed. 'It's the ritual of this world. But every husband is a unique burden, and I can tell you your father was a relatively bearable burden. It's all your husband's fault, not yours, I would say, because boys tend to imitate their father. Your father used to say that if Ahmad wasn't as big as he was, he would have gone and kicked his balls twice. But your husband was too strong, huge. Nobody could hope to kick his balls and get back home with limbs intact. But don't worry,' she said, 'God is there, planning it all out.'

'Of course.' I could only sigh.

I remember returning home, thinking confused thoughts, blaming God for fathering all these hardships, for authoring my fate, and all night I blamed God for each little thing. I dredged up long forgotten misfortunes so that I could hate God a little more. And this is what I hated most about God: that he always sides with men. That he is He. But nowhere is there a more confused bitch than Nabeesu, for I was up early the next morning offering the predawn prayers, filled with guilt, genuflecting with repentance, willing to accept whatever God had in store for me with pious indifference. I assured God that I would never again complain but read the Quran quietly at the dawn of dawn and accept whatever fate had in store for me with daughterly obedience. But I expected punishment anyway for I had hated God and I had blasphemed. I had faulted him for every little sorrow, my tongue had ridiculed him, cussing him for being He and not She, calling him a dumb insensitive power, useless like my husband, and I expected punishment anyway because what is God without punishment? Life has always been a dumb music and I could only expect it to grow dumber.

When they came, I was in the dining room, counting the leaking holes in the roof, my mind full of confused thoughts. They knocked on the door. At first I thought it was the latch lashing in the wind. But then the knocks acquired a human quality, a few persistent impatient knuckles on the door. It couldn't have been my children. It couldn't have been my husband. When I began to move towards the door, the knocking ceased, and when I pulled the door open, they were there. Three men clothed in white, young and tall and bearded like my own sons, were seated in the plastic chairs outside. Another man, with a turban as white as his beard wrapped around his head the way some imams wear it, stood a few feet from the door, staring. I pulled the shawl over my head and tucked it behind my ears.

I said, 'Please, be seated.'

Those who were seated rose from their chairs and the older man stepped away from me, visibly angry.

'You couldn't tame him,' he said, 'now mend him before it's too late.'

'Tame and mend whom?' I said. 'And before it's too late for what?'

'Burhan,' he said.

'Mend his ways,' one of the young men said.

'Before it's too late to mend,' the other young man said,

coming towards me, his lips stuttering and his voice fluctuating with rage.

My heart raced and I felt scared and provoked at the same time. 'You are louder than you need to be.'

'Sounds like his mother only,' the third said, rushing towards me from the corner as their father looked on with his hand on the wall.

'Will you cool down,' I said, 'please? Don't behave as if I know what you are talking about.'

'Burhan,' the man said, pushing his son aside. 'I don't want the neighbourhood to throng here on a Friday and I haven't come here to match my temper with a shrew anyway. Isn't he home?'

I was stunned and couldn't gather myself immediately. The man pushed me aside and barged into the dining room followed by his boys and went raiding room after room. I met them in the kitchen. Steady streams from the roof-holes fell into the bowls and buckets and mugs scattered all over the floor and they stood amidst them, pitying the house, pitying my fate, and my fate was this house, this leaking house, and the men in it.

'Where is Burhan?'

'He isn't home yet from the mosque, but please,' I said, 'tell me what it is. What has my child done?' The way they were talking and looking, the way they were moving around, dampened my eyes with worry and my voice was breaking with dread.

'How come he isn't home? He was one of the first to leave the mosque. How come he isn't home yet?'

'How do you know he was one of the first to leave the mosque? Were you stalking my son? Are you from around here? What has he done?'

'Or is he already where he needs to be?'

'Where is that?'

They were all staring at me, as if I knew what it was all about. My cheeks quivered and my heart jumped like a fish out of water and my temperature was rising. They scrambled across the dining room towards the front door. They collected and opened their umbrellas, their eight eyes staring at me. Outside the trees were falling and leaves were blowing wild and running indoors and and thunderbolts tore through the darkened day like some circus of the Almighty. They turned to go.

I said, 'Please, what has my son done? You can't leave me like this.'

But they went out of the house and I couldn't help but go after them, careful not to slip but slipping nonetheless, scrambling to find my slippers and not finding them, worrying about what my child had done to them, afraid of what they might do to my child for they looked really upset, really serious, really strong, men who were capable of rage beyond their control.

I repeated, 'Please, you have to tell me what my son has done. You can't leave me like this.'

The men said nothing. They switched open their big fancy umbrellas and stepped out into the rain, one after the other, and I stepped out after them, barefoot, asking them what it was that my child had done, what offence he had committed. They were walking really fast and I had to run, seeking an explanation to this drama. Then the young men stopped on the trail. The young men stopped because their old man stopped. His face was frothing with anger. A face that wanted no speaking done in the rain. And then he took two steps backwards and I couldn't see his face any more. It was raining harder and harder and such was the wind that I could hardly stop blinking and green leaves were blowing all around us and I was without an umbrella.

The rain was deafening, so he spoke as loud as he could because I couldn't have heard him otherwise. He cried, 'I warned him in clear terms not to knock on Reyhana's door. With or without her invitation.'

'Who is Reyhana?'

'My sister-in-law. My brother Sadique's wife.'

'The one who is in the Gulf?'

'My name's Saud,' he said, 'and these are my sons. Tell your son we came looking for him. Tell him we came looking for him to kill him.'

'Kill him? Kill him? But why? What are you talking about?'

'Will your brothers approve of your running an affair outside the marriage with a boy fifteen years your junior?' he said. 'What will they do to him?'

I couldn't say anything at all and my whole being froze. He turned and walked away. I ran and blocked his way and beseeched him not to harm my boy. He asked me to give him his way. I didn't. So he took the tip of his mundu and shoved it under his armpit. He shifted his umbrella from his right hand to his left hand. Then he put his free hand on my shoulder and kind of pushed me. The trail was slippery and the man was big and strong. Even a gentle push was enough for me and I slipped and tripped and fell butt-down in a puddle of mud. He regarded me indifferently for a couple of seconds and then walked away, followed by his sons, all of them stooping under their umbrellas to shield themselves from the storm. I got up on my feet. My hips hurt and my wrists stiffened from the shock of the fall, began to swell. Inside me, my confusions and worries rioted. I closed my eyes. Standing in the rain. Pitying my peaceless existence. When I opened my eyes, they were there, under a small umbrella, Ashraf and Hakimaakka. I said nothing. I turned and shambled back home. I scrambled in the house for Imran's phone and rang Burhan. His phone was switched off.

Chinnan

We were having sex, Panchami and I, when Damu began knocking on the door. We sighed in frustration and lay on our backs, listening to the rain.

'This is what happens when you have a child that loves you too much,' she whispered. 'The child won't let you fuck in peace.'

'I suppose so,' I agreed. Damu was a particularly difficult case.

Damu kept on knocking. We put on clothes. I went and unbolted the door to let him in, but he didn't come in. Aren't they complex things, children? He just stood there like a wounded lover, staring into the room. I unhooked my shirt from the wall and went out to the kitchen and put on the wide palm-frond hat, which was my father's or my father's father's, an heirloom from antiquity.

My son was behind me, I knew. Staring accusingly. I could feel it. So I told him what my father once told me.

'Damu, my father once told me that there are only a few things in the world more exciting than catfishing and turtling. But we won't do either catfishing or turtling today,' I said, feeling the stare of his eyes, which were his mother's eyes, sad and dark and blazing. 'Instead, we will do some eeling.'

We stood by the door, watching the rain. I stepped out into the rain with Damu, I in my palm-frond hat and the boy under a pink umbrella made ugly by all those butterfly stickers you get free with chewing gums. I walked with my boy, my stubborn boy, wanting to come out with his father all the time, no matter the weather. We walked in silence towards the paddy fields. I dug up some earthworms and a whorl of clay at the banana plantations and wrapped them in a teak leaf. I stopped on the culvert over the stream at the beginning of the fields and fished out a crumpled cigarette from my shirt pocket and lit it. Even the smoke tasted like carom seeds. I took another puff and threw the butt into the water below and took my boy's hand and went west on the wall that divided the stream from the paddy fields. Some distance down, I asked him to give me an earthworm. He opened the teak leaf and broke the big morsel of clay full of earthworms and gave me one.

'Give me a bigger one.'

His fingers went jostling in the morsel of clay and came out with a bigger worm.

'Good.'

He folded the teak leaf once again. I stuck the fishing rod under my arm and pulled the worm on to the hook neatly like a condom and cut off the rest of it and gave it back to him. He held the squirming half of the worm in his palm and then dropped it into the stream. I grinned at him. He didn't grin back. I tilted my hat a little onto my shoulder and stepped down into the water with the hook in hand. I looked for holes in the mossy wall above the water level. There were freshwater snails, drenched in their yellow shells, and I plucked one off the wall. I took the worm off the hook and then broke the shell of the mollusc in my palm with the heel of my hand. Then I hooked the slippery thing.

I was nipple-deep in the water, the current strong and cold and the bed of the stream weedy and clayey. But I plodded on, almost swam, up the stream looking for a hole where a tire-track eel might be hiding, waiting for my bait. I saw a hole and pushed the hook deep into it with the rod. I climbed out of the stream, the rod in hand. My lungi had turned a deep brown, the colour of the water, the colour of the fields that were algae-green only a week ago when the dark clouds hadn't yet rumbled their way over the hills from the Arabian Sea. I put a rock on the rod to secure it and looked for Damu. He wasn't where he was supposed to be. I gave a shout down the stream, useless though it was in the downpour. But I shouted anyway and heard the boy's voice somewhere behind me. I turned around and walked up the stream in the mood to scold. The current was scary and the boy was small. Twelve years old. He was emerging from the middle of an overflowing irrigation ditch. I approached him to reproach him because he was wet from head to feet. He was holding the umbrella strenuously between the neck and shoulder to keep it from flying off because it was windy now, the areca palms were beginning to bend. But I couldn't scold him. In his hand was one big banded snakehead, its head clasped shut in his palm, its tail thrashing ceaselessly against his small arms. He stood with a faint smirk on his face. And that accusing look he had in his eyes when I opened the door to him after fucking his mother. My wife. I couldn't look him in the eye. I couldn't scold him. I broke a sprig of jungle geranium that stood nearby and grabbed the snakehead from him and stuck the sprig up its gill and started for home, crying, 'Hurry up, Damu.'

Damu walked past me and ran up the stairs that led to the road and stood on the culvert, waiting for me. Or so I thought. When I reached him, Damu pointed a finger along the road, across the fields, saying nothing. That's how I saw Burhan.

Reyhana

He didn't go to aunt Nishiya because aunt Nishiya would ask him to do something, perhaps to go to the ration shop to buy kerosene or wheat, or to the flourmill to grind coriander seeds. He didn't go to aunt Sulaikha because he knew aunt Sulaikha had four sacks of areca nuts to husk and if he went there, he would have to sit down with her and husk them, smelling the wet-tobacco stench of those husks and the nuts inside he so hated. He didn't go to aunt Rukhiyya because aunt Rukhiyya would bore him with her restless tongue, with the same old stories and jokes that were not jokes but endless gripes about her son, his cousin Zaman, and he was in no mood to subject himself to that. He didn't go to aunt Sumaiyya because aunt Sumaiyya adored him so much she wouldn't let him go before lunch.

But there was no reason why he went up the hill.

Up the hill—its highpoint a little bed of shiny black rocks still wet from the morning drizzle, surrounded on all four sides by the lush green grass that was at least twice as tall as him. He stood on a balancing rock that rose right from the middle of the bed of rocks, breathing heavily. He thrashed the tall grass on both sides to a slant with a stick he had picked up in the lower woods and the valley opened up before him, towards the west, where the river flowed and our villages and town stood—white specks of matchbox structures scattered up the slopes of minor hills along the banks. The valley itself was an undulation of hills, palm country, verdant in the pre-monsoon showers of a late April precisely sixteen monsoons ago. He watched the valley far below in awe, scanning for a hint of where his home stood, but all he could see were the isolated columns of white kitchen smoke rising above this coconut-hatted country. He imagined his mother to be somewhere on this side of the paddy fields, along the banks where the river bent deeply under the bridge and disappeared into the green dense undulant wilderness. He turned back and looked east, thrashing the grass to left and right. Hills extended endlessly and disappeared into the cerulean blue of the sky, the valley deeper and denser and without human settlements, or so it seemed to him because no spires of smoke rose even though the valley was coconut-hatted still and indistinguishably similar to the view of our own valley to the west. Sans the river and the town, of course. From where he stood, everything was below him, and he felt afraid. He fastened his lungi and skidded down the balancing rock and thrashed his way down through the grass, now at least thrice as tall as him, through the fresh trail his climbing had made.

He was nine then and that was the story he had told Tresya eight years later, standing tall in a large raincoat on the balancing rock while the clouds broke in a tremendous pelter and gusts blew from the north and soundless lightning lit up the grey world in brilliant neon blues and Tresya shuddered, tightened her arms around his waist, leaning on her toes and rubbing her cheeks against his cheeks, her round hard palmable breasts enlarging and pressing more firmly against his wet chest with every soft nervous sigh, warm even in that cool midsummer rain. She was really in the mood for her first kiss but, instead of sharing the moment's romance, Burhan lowered himself and took one of her nipples through the blouse in his mouth and bit. Sharply. And Tresya punished the indiscipline. Her slap was accompanied by a blast of thunder and lightning that ran like a fire-serpent down the valley. He could see it because the slap was also accompanied by a furious kick at his feet and he had fallen, skidding down from the rock into the bed of smaller rocks and sharp-bladed grass below. And that was the story he told me these eight years later when he came home from the mosque, laughing gaily at the memory.

He lay on his back and I lay on top of him, listening, looking intently, studiously into the flickering flame in the centre of his deep brown eyes where my own body was somehow visible to me in all its milk. I tried to remember what I was doing at the time when Burhan had taken Tresya up the hill, all the slippery way up that damn steep hill, sometimes even carrying her on his back, or so he told me, to help her discover God's view of our valley he had discovered when he was a mere nine-year-old boy.

I remembered that I was precisely thirty-two years old at the time, already a mother to two teen girls, girls who owed no semblance to their father whom I wouldn't have married when I was only fifteen if he had not gone to the Gulf and made all the money he was making at that time. I, the daughter of a poor climber of areca palms, couldn't have insisted on choosing the right match for myself. Nor could I have expected my parents to deliver me a marriage with someone who was both rich and handsome. Sadique was rich, wanted nothing in dowry, and had promised to build a house in my name. I had thought about the offer for days and I was convinced that financial security couldn't be compromised for a handsomer face. Besides, my mother had told me that a woman's way in the world is always difficult. So I let him marry me when I was fifteen. Even though he was as sentimental as a dog. Even though he was dark as a crow and this was a concern. Of course, my mother agreed. But you get used to everything, she said, looking at her husband, my father, as though she were pointing out an instance. You get used to everything but money, she said. That's one mighty lack to get used to. But, lying on top of Burhan, looking deeply into his deep brown eyes, it seemed to me that my mother was not entirely right. She was right to a great extent, but not entirely. There are things other than money that give a marriage its desirability and sustainability. Gentleness in care, a healthy emotional bond, a little mutual liking, a sense of togetherness without being adhesively dependent, some space and some freedom of air. Yes, my mother was right to a great extent, I think so. I would have divorced him for sure if I were rich. With my milky skin I could still have fetched some bald widower less dark and not a lot older than Sadique. After all, I wouldn't have had to marry him if I were born to a father with better means.

So, yes, my mother was right about the crucial role of money, its blanket of security, but not entirely. Certainly not to the extent that one could forsake one's bodily needs for eternity, its yearning for beauty, its desire for touch, to love and to be loved. The marriage needed some dose of sexual unburdening. Your dumb body knows it even before your wise mind figures it out. In the long nights I grew lonely, my skin grew feverous even before my mind knew anything about it, longing sleeplessly for the unemotional, irresponsible, liberating company of a man who was not my husband.

That was roughly how my life was going when seventeen-year-old Burhan ascended the hill with Tresya, Dorothy Teacher's daughter, a girl two years older than him. And if the disease hadn't come my way, I might well have had my way. But that wasn't to be. The disease came, the body grew weak. The disease went away, leaving my body stuck with his kidney, leaving a long J-scar round my belly, and all the fever began to ebb from my skin. Instead, there was now a thick layer of mud all over my skin. The mud of all the discontents of this dull marriage. Energy drained from my body and I grew numb, lethargic, hopeless, almost menopausal. And that was my state until some four months ago when I met Burhan for the first time: I was living my lifeless life in a loveless marriage. But, then, when I met him, met Burhan for the first time, all the fever of my pre-transplantation thirties was right back on my skin, only far more intensely, almost burning.

Four months ago.

I had gone to the travel agency in Areekode to collect my passport with the visa for Umrah. There he was at the counter, standing in for his friends who had gone out for tea or something. He had a face that instantly left me tactless with longing. With long hair neatly roached to the back from the broad forehead and a youthful beard shining with that virginal shine of new manhood. His shoulders were close-set and he had hairy arms.

And brown eyes, half innocent and somehow half voluptuous, made more intense by the faintly purplish surma that shadowed them. His eyes had a way of looking that liked being looked at. His skin was a pure, irresistible ripe-tamarind brown, just like his eyes. I can't explain in words the sheer charm of him except that in me desire took wings and rose from some deep repressed region inside me like a bird. He was ridiculously handsome. He looked far too young for me, far too tall, but I couldn't care less. So I threw out in sentences my years of frustration. Like cheap postcards seeking desperate communication. Like one of those buxom aunties in the second-rate Malayalam smut in the second-rate magazines of the nineties.

I said, 'Who do you have those from?'

'What?'

'Your eyes.'

His eyes looked uncertain and askant. Then he fixed his eyes on mine for a moment before looking away. 'Nabeesu.'

'That's your mother?'

'That's right.'

'She must be really beautiful.' I felt worse than a slut.

'She is okay.'

'I see. Why are you wearing a denim shirt in this hot weather?'

He turned again to look into my eyes, puzzled.

So I said, 'With a cotton or even linen shirt, maybe you won't have to keep your buttons open.' What's the superlative of slut? That's what I felt like.

He still looked puzzled. So I asked him to continue rummaging the shelves for my passport. The puzzled look remained as he said he was not sure where Arif and Rafeed—his friends who owned the agency and who had gone out—had kept my passport.

'You will have to wait till Arif comes back,' he said, buttoning up his shirt.

'How long will I have to wait?

'Half an hour maybe.'

'Where do you live?'

'Vaiga.'

'That's why. You looked vaguely familiar. Well, that's not far from my house. My house is right across the paddy fields. The first house on the left after the fields, a double-storey house painted in white.'

'I think I know your house.'

'Ah. So you have seen it. It's difficult to miss if you pass by daily. Anyway, would you be kind enough to deliver the passport to my home on your way back, please? I can't wait till your friends come back. It's too hot to wait.'

'Sure, Thaatha. And even if I forget to deliver it, you can just cross over to Vaiga and collect it from my home. I am Nabeesu's youngest.'

'You are what?'

'Nabeesu's youngest.'

'What is your name?'

'Burhan,' he said. 'You cross the stream and walk some three or four hundred metres up the trail by the temple before turning left along the cashew plantations on the trail towards the granite quarries. After the quarries, you turn right and my home is just twenty paces down. That's the short cut. Or else you can take the main road and ask anyone at the Bazaar and they would be able to direct you.'

'That sounds near enough,' I said, with a fake sigh.

Finally he managed to shed the puzzled curiosity from his eyes and smiled a sly-shy little smile. 'I am sorry. I am a forgetful type. And quite lazy.'

'Well,' I said, 'let's test that out,' and left without turning back.

It turned out that he was indeed forgetful. Two days had passed and my passport hadn't reached me. I didn't want to, but on the third day I phoned the travel agency, and Arif or Rafeed told me that my passport was with Burhan. One of them told me that it had been with Burhan for the past two days. So I cut the call, thanking him, and decided to continue waiting. By evening he was at my doorstep, opting to knock even though the buzzer was on the wall right beside the door. When I opened the door, he was there, with my passport stamped with the visa, wearing a white mundu and maroon round-necked T-shirt, smiling either awkwardly or apologetically, almost blushing. I invited him inside for tea, but he refused to enter. He said he had to hurry somewhere and slipped into his slippers.

'Next time,' he said, refusing to look me in the eyes.

I said nothing. I decided to wait. I heard nothing from him for two months. I thought I had forgotten him but I hadn't. Because, when two months later I received a *Hello* on my mobile phone from an anonymous number, I knew it was him.

How old are you, Burhan? I texted back, right away.

Twenty-five, he replied.

Well, I had to think what I wanted to type, *well*, I typed, *I am forty and you know what?*

What? he wrote back.

That was Khadijah's age when she married Muhammad, I typed. *It's strange why I even thought about it*. It was true. It was strange. I don't know why I wrote that.

That's strange, he texted back, with one of those rolling-eyes emojis.

I didn't know what to text next. After a minute, I typed, *Exactly my thought*, and sent.

And so began our chats from morning to midnight, and it took me two more nights to finally persuade him to come home. I could see his flashlight down in the paddy fields coming towards my home in the middle of the night as I waited for him on my balcony without any light. Wanting to be with him but afraid. Very afraid. Afraid that someone might see him and I couldn't imagine the consequences. I told him to skip the main road and take the trail along the paddy fields, cross over, jump the wall and enter the house from behind through the kitchen. I had kept the kitchen door unlocked. I had also told him not to use a flashlight. It was too dark to see, of course, but it would be safer without the flashlight, I had told him. But there he was, with a flashlight in hand. I ran my eyes in every direction anxiously, looking for a shadow or faint trace of any other light, and when he reached, I was more relieved than happy. And then I was happy. But also nervous to the core and ashamed of it a bit, facing a boy fifteen years younger, later feeling him and being felt, sweating naked on the marine-blue sheets, our limbs locked for hours, as I fucked away two decades of sexual privation.

It all began idly. Like some exquisite trouble.

At first it was like fucking for the sake of fucking. It was freedom. But the terror of being found out grew in me each time he left home for me, each time he left me for home, from the first moment I saw his flashlight in the dark till the last moment it vanished into the same dark place across the stream that it came from. An illicit affair courted consequences. And the way we were carrying on ours, night after night, coupled with the sheer offence of our age-difference, made this illicit affair all the more ominous. But with the persistent fear of being found out also grew a kind of passionate dependence and I grew afraid of that as well. Because he was everything my husband was not and I grew sleepless in the nights. And, besides, I often remembered what my mother had told me, that one's way in the world is made hellish without money. She was right in that, I knew, and I was not prepared to wager away the financial security that my husband gave me. I was not prepared to lose my children either, or to wake one morning having metamorphosed overnight into that bitch of future village legends who opened her doors for a boy fifteen years younger. I decided not to fall in love with him, but passion grew in me despite the effort, just like terror grew in me, the terror of being found out. My heart and my mind wavered between desire and fear. I succumbed to fear. So, a week ago, I made a tremendous effort and told him not to come home any more. I told him I had grown afraid of the nights. He was quiet about it, understanding. And I was quiet about it. Or so I thought until today when he messaged me from the mosque and then I understood that it all was disquiet. I succumbed to desire and I couldn't resist texting back. I wanted to meet him then and I wanted him beside me right away. So I told him to come home because the day was dark as any dark night in the terrible rain and there was no one around anywhere. Not even the birds.

Shahid

I walked home with the Imam, saying nothing.

My house was further up the slope, a few minutes' walk north from the mosque. We got home drenched in the rain despite the size of our umbrellas and even my father got a little wet when he opened the door for us. He sneezed as he shut the door behind us and then broke into a coughing fit. The Imam wanted to say something but now he waited for my father to finish coughing. My father sat down on a chair and we watched him until his coughing ceased. It was a relatively short fit, which sometimes lasted as long as five minutes. Those scary fits always left me with the sick feeling that they would be his last even though I knew they couldn't be. He had been coughing for as long as I could remember. He told me that he had started coughing at least two years before he started smoking. He started smoking at thirteen, as a worker at the communist beedi company, where even the women smoked.

The fit lasted no more than two minutes this time and then he was able to breathe normally again, looking up at the Imam, lighting a beedi with the air of someone who had never once coughed in his life. With the joy of someone who had just been introduced to smoking. My mother appeared at the kitchen door with an emergency light and two towels, one for the Imam and one for me. I put the emergency light in the middle of the dining table and extended one towel to the Imam but he refused. He took off his turban and placed it on top of the TV console, dragged up a chair and sat down facing my father. The rain dripped from the Imam's wet mundu and legs and snaked across the floor towards the sofa.

My father looked at it and then looked up at the Imam and said, 'Maybe you need to dry yourself a little bit.'

'Forget it,' the Imam said. 'Not since 1991. What do you say?'

'What do I say about what?'

'1991.'

'What do I say about 1991? The rain?'

'What else? It's beginning to turn frightening.'

'Is it? I don't think my memory is any good when it comes to the weather.'

'Didn't get a peek when you opened the door for us?'

My father said nothing. Outside the weather was now stormy. We could hear the wind and the thunder. The Imam went and opened the door to have a look and then closed it. His face was radiant with excitement. He said, 'Your coconut tree is bending in the storm just as you were a moment ago.'

'Butt up,' I said.

Only I was laughing. My mother turned at the door and went back to the kitchen. I could hear her pull the steel plates, cups, spoons and ladles from the rack with all the usual violence as she prepared to serve us lunch.

'Don't joke about my lungs,' my father said. 'That's no joking matter. The coconut tree has been bending that way every monsoon as far back as I can remember, just as I have been coughing my dry coughs even before I had any memory. Rest assured, despite all the bending, we will both last. It does look a bit bleaker than the last June though, I must say.' He leant forward and I thought he was going to cough again. He put his hand down his waist and brought it out with something between his thumb and forefinger.

'Bed bug,' he said. 'They have taken to touring the most unholy regions of my body ever since the onset of monsoon.'

I dragged a chair forward and sat down at the dining table. A twig mantis climbed the emergency light like the skeleton of some dream creature. My mother placed on the table the plates of rice and saucers with sardine cooked with black pepper, ginger and dried gooseberries. There were also shrimp chammanthi, mango chutney, tamarind-ginger sauce and fried mackerel. She brought a jug of lukewarm cumin-seed water along with three glasses and a bowl of naadan chicken curry with two ladles and three spoons. And then she stood looking at us, hands on hips. *Eat your damned feast*, she seemed to say.

Each household under the jurisdiction of our mosque had to feed the Imam one week every six months on a rotational basis. My mother hated these compulsory feasts. So she said to the Imam, 'It's high time they began paying you in cash, not in kind.'

My father backed her up. 'It must be awkward even for you to keep eating your food in a different house every week. There is little dignity to speak of in knocking on someone's door for one's hard-earned food. What do you think, Shahnavaz?'

The Imam was just beginning to mouth the big ball of rice in his palm but he didn't. He grew visibly uneasy. Even I grew uneasy because you are not supposed to make your guest uneasy at the dining table. So I asked my parents to shut up. They did. We ate in silence.

Then I was thinking, eating and thinking. About my wifeless afternoons and lonelier nights. Remembering. I could have remarried after she deserted me a couple of years ago but I hadn't because I didn't trust women any more. I still don't. *Women so fleshy and fuckable and fickle and fake and faithless and fallible and fragile and so driven by and to the pleasures of the skin. Women so beautiful and so hairless. Women so pitifully weak, yet so full of loud cowardice and empty venom and vicious betrayals, controlled by men in their acts of hot defiance as in their cold obedience.* It's not the bitch I was remembering but the betrayal, the child that it deprived me of, the child that was of me alone and looked like me until the day she left home. Once she left home, once the shock began to ebb, my part in my child's face also ebbed, day by day, until, in less than a week, the child was a complete stranger. I was gone from the child's face like half the moon on the seventh night. The mother's part in his face was certainly his mother's but the father's part wasn't mine. That's why I didn't chase her down. That's why I let the child go. Also, my mother told me that a child without its mother wasn't the same as a child without its father. But the decision to let the child go was certainly mine, not my mother's.

I turned my phone on.

My father belched loudly. I knew it was meant to disgust the Imam. The Imam knew it, too. And we also knew that my father would belch even louder now. We waited for it. I saw my father labour about his throat to belch more, but he couldn't. His Adam's apple stopped wiggling and stilled. Mother appeared at the door and went round the table, looking down at the soiled floor, and then went back and stood at the door, glowering at us all. Like, *Eat your damned feast.*

My phone rang.

Chinnan was calling. I took the call. Chinnan said he saw

Burhan crossing the fields towards Reyhana's house on his secret business once again. This is what he had told me a few days ago too, before the rain. That he saw Burhan on a secret business at Reyhana's house. I had told him then to tell me whenever he happened to see Burhan near Reyhana's house again, no matter the time, no matter the weather.

Chinnan told me what he saw and then he went silent on the phone, waiting for me to say something in response. But I couldn't say anything at all. Because Burhan had left the mosque only a few minutes before we had left and I couldn't believe what Chinnan was saying.

I looked at the Imam, who was busy eating. I had a morsel of rice in my own hand, but now I dropped it back on the plate and stood up.

This can't be allowed in our village, I told him. This business of visiting the mother of two adult girls when their father is toiling in a faraway desert, I told him, this can't be allowed. What are we men for if we can't even take care of a lecherous son of a bitch among us who is not even bothered by her age? I said, What kind of a bitch is she who isn't even bothered by the age of the son of a bitch she is naked with right now, forgetful about the honour of her husband who is slaving his life away in the faraway deserts of Arabia. And this, on a holy Friday noon?

That's when the light came on and I realised their eyes were watching me: the Imam's, my father's, my mother's. But I couldn't care less. There is value in life, I told Chinnan. It's an insult to the honour of all our brothers toiling in the boiling deserts. This time we can't let him go. I told him to keep circulating the news, whether via WhatsApp or through calls or in person. I cut the call. I turned on the internet and typed up the story quickly and sent it on three or four WhatsApp groups popular among boys in the village. And then I called some of them.

June

We were waiting for Ippa. He went out as soon as he came in. And then we were waiting for him again. It felt like a long time. It was still windy and I could hear the trees. The day was like a black-and-white movie on a black-and-white TV. Dull and blurry. It was like a sea raging on the roof. With the rain roaring in the roaring wind. The candle flame was still and steady. Blue. Frustration was visible in Imma's eyes, the frustration of waiting so long for Ippa. Imma's eyes were growing less blue. She wanted to have lunch and she never had lunch without Ippa. Ippa wouldn't like it either if Imma ate without him. They liked having lunch together so they could talk to each other and their lunches lasted long. Almost an hour. Imma's eyes were in my eyes and it bothered me. So I turned and looked at the candle. The wax candle had melted beautifully and the flame was thin without the wick, wavering. The flame went out when Ippa opened the door. Again. Imma stood up from her chair, not because Ippa had come in but because this time he wasn't alone. This time Hakimaakka was with him. They were drenched like those seals on Animal Planet. Imma put her shawl over her head and looked at them, confused.

'Why are you both so drenched?' Imma said to Ippa.

'That would make a long story.'

'Like what? You haven't been out for long enough at all to come back with a long story.'

'Looks like some trouble is up for Nabeesumma and family.'

'Stop talking to yourself and say it for what it is,' Imma said.

I asked Hakimaakka to close the door because the wind was blowing the rain inside. But he didn't close the door. 'Did you offer your Friday prayer, June?' he asked me. 'Don't you go to the mosque with your father?'

'I am too young to pray and too old to go to the mosque,' I said.

'Well,' he said, 'a lot of girls older than you do.'

'Well, girls from my mother's side don't.'

He said nothing.

Imma was watching Ippa and Ippa looked worried and confused and excited at the same time.

'Four men, not from around here, have come on a visit to Nabeesumma's,' Ippa said to Imma.

'Yes, I saw them pass some time ago.'

'And then?' From Ippa's eyes the worry and confusion were gone. Now only excitement remained.

Imma said, 'Then what? I had gone out to the porch. They were four of them, maybe a father and his three sons. They saw me and asked where Nabeesumma's house was and I told them. What happened?'

Confusion was back in Ippa's eyes. But excitement was there, too. He was dripping like a wet sloth bear. His moustache was like a wet black worm right under his nose. His moustache was quivering because his lips were quivering. Hakimaakka went out and stood on the porch, looking out towards the trail. Ippa stared at Hakimaakka for a beat and then continued speaking to Imma, 'Well, then what? Remember I came in and then went out again?'

'God, go ahead with your story, please, will you?' Imma's eyes were blue-blue with curiosity. 'I am listening.'

'Well, I went out because I heard a tree crash at Hakimaakka's side. I wanted to see which tree it was this time around. That's when I saw Nabeesumma and the four men. They were out on the trail. She was without an umbrella, you see? And she was chasing them and blocking them. As if pleading. And I saw one of them slap Nabeesumma. Twice.'

'Slap Nabeesumma?' Imma said, with exaggerated disbelief. But I could see that Imma believed in the story despite the shock of disbelief in her face.

Hakimaakka came back in and went out again to watch the trail.

'And you did nothing?' Imma said. 'Did you talk to Nabeesumma? Is she all right?' Imma was beginning to worry now. Her worried eyes were a little less blue than her believing eyes.

Ippa was coughing. Ippa was coughing and not talking. He was dripping like a pile of wet umbrellas.

'You are going to come down with a fever.' She undraped her hair again and gave the shawl to Ippa. 'Dry yourself.'

Ippa went on coughing as if he had swallowed a fly or a mosquito and the insect was stuck in his throat. He coughed like he wanted to eject something from his throat.

I said, 'Ippa, did you swallow a fly? Ippa, did you swallow a mosquito?' But Ippa didn't answer. So I turned to Imma, 'Imma, are we going to have lunch anytime soon?'

But Imma didn't answer either. I couldn't blame them. They were all so engrossed in the tale of Nabeesumma and the four strangers. One of them, according to Ippa, had slapped her. Twice. Ippa wasn't drying his head because he was coughing, so Imma started drying his hair with her shawl. So Ippa was coughing and Imma was drying Ippa's head. It was funny to watch because neither liked what the other was doing. But when Hakimaakka came back and called to him, Ippa's coughing ceased and Imma stopped drying his head.

'Imran and Ibrahim are coming,' Hakimaakka said, gasping a little.

Ippa went out and Imma went after him. I got up from my chair finally and went up to the door and discovered that it wasn't raining any more. The wind was gone. I wondered why I hadn't realised it before. I think I was busy hating the rain so much that I didn't realise when it ceased raining. It was pleasantly shocking. I could hear toads crying from every hole and corner. Happy bellyful cries. *Paaakroww Paaakroww Paaakroww.* The water was swirling about our front yard and rushing down the slope towards the backyard. I saw Ippa and Hakimaakka wade across the yard knee-deep in the water shouting *Imraaan Imraaan Imraaan.*

They were all in a hurry. Within seconds they were gone. I could only see Imma standing knee-deep in the water watching Ippa and Hakimaakka. Like a black-and-white scene from some black-and-white movie.

Imran

We left for home a few minutes after Ashraf did, Ibrahim and I.

'It's not going to stop storming any time soon,' Ibrahim said.

The porch of the mosque was jam-packed. I didn't have my umbrella, Burhan had taken it. So Ibrahim took me under his. I turned around for a second, folding my mundu, looking for Dulqar and Rashid, our younger brothers, but couldn't find them in the crowd.

The weather was bleak. It was like rain plus eclipse. The weather was beginning to get on my nerves. Giving me the jitters and mood swings. Like I was on my menses or something. The weather was causing Imma's mood swings, too. The leaking roof and all.

Imma always had mood swings. (You are on an eternal period, Nabeesu, Ippa would often say to Imma.) But during the monsoon her moods took extreme swings, understandable because she was living in a house with a leaking roof and five non-working sons who wouldn't let her rest even at this age. With a husband who could, Imma would say, with one casual look on the first of January render the whole year useless for everyone he sets his eyes on. The thing about the quarrels between Imma and Ippa was that you got to hear a lot of funny things. But they were not always funny. Only two weeks ago Imma had unleashed a rant over a tarp for the kitchen at the end of which she had called him a deflated dick. Now that's not the nicest way to talk in front of your own children. But then that's not her, not really, but the other her, the one in the extremities of her mood swings, her seasonal double. In the monsoons her mood swings were unpredictable. But most of the time Imma is calm. Calm and working. Reciting the Quran and praying five times a day. Ensuring three good meals a day for all the non-working adults in the house under her care. As though she were running some day-care centre for adults. She doesn't talk much when she is calm and her big loud presence in the house would become as small as her body when she resigned to silence. It would be as if the air had gone blank in the shape of Nabeesumma. A mechanical blank that spoke nothing.

I was thinking of Imma because I was thinking of the weather and the weather was getting on my nerves, too. We were wet till the waist even though the umbrella was big, a new four-fold Popy.

The roadside stank of rotten cashew fruits from the orchards, green and red and yellow. The wind had blown away the corrugated iron-sheet roofing of the communists' red-painted bus stop and the life-sized wooden Che Guevera who had towered over the bus stop an hour ago now lay flat on the road, minus one arm. I looked at Ibrahim and Ibrahim looked at me. We lifted Che Guevra off the road and placed him against the bus-stop wall, where he slid in the wind once more and flumped sideways, breaking the other arm. We left him there and walked on.

Four men passed us on the trail that led to our home from the main road. They were perfect strangers. But the way they regarded us, briefly but intensely, stirred something in me, bruised something in me. I tugged at the scruff of Ibrahim's shirt and we stood looking at them until they got into a Willys parked at the Bazaar under the carob tree. I waited to see if they would start the vehicle and drive away but they didn't.

'Do you know them?'

'No,' I said.

'So why are you looking at them like that?'

'Don't they look like trouble, Ikka?'

'Sure they do,' he said, 'the way they were looking at us and all. I noticed that. But why should we bother if the trouble isn't ours. Come, let's get going.'

So we continued homewards through the flooded trail. But their faces lingered in my mind, their look bruised something like pride in me although they hadn't done or said anything. For some reason the look of them didn't augur well.

I can sense trouble faster than a serpent.

The trail was strewn with rotten leaves and broken branches and we were struggling to keep the umbrella from flying off. Then the miracle happened. The rain ceased and the wind slowed down. There were two consecutive mighty claps of thunder and then there were none for a few moments. Lightning scrawled across the sky in soundless explosions and then there were none for a few moments. It felt like a blessed waking from the spectacle of a long dream.

'That's quite a respite,' Ibrahim said.

'Amazing,' I said. 'This goddamned rain was getting on my nerves. On Imma's nerves, too.'

We were ankle-deep in the water. Brown dirty water. It only got better when we began to go up the slope through Ashraf's land.

'Ibrahim, Imran.'

That was Ashraf's voice, calling us from behind. We turned around but we could only see the blind bend where the trail sloped steeply. We could hear his voice, not see him. And then he emerged, labouring up the slope, waving a hand. For some reason I thought of the four strangers who had crossed our path and their red Willys. My mood swung into a cautious quiet.

I can sense trouble faster than a serpent.

'I owe him some two thousand rupees,' Ibrahim said.

'It doesn't look like that's what he's after in this weather, Ikka.'

'Then one of our trees must have crashed on his fence.'

'Maybe,' I said, but I didn't mean it. Because it felt like a different kind of trouble, going by the faces that had crossed our path. I saw Hakimaakka also emerge from the cover of the slope on the curve, just behind Ashraf. 'Maybe not.'

Both of them were jogging towards us. I knew the trouble was ours.

I can sense trouble faster than a still serpent.

Ibrahim looked puzzled, assured now that the money he owed Ashraf wasn't the issue here. Nor a tree that had crashed in the crazy wind right across his bamboo fence, destroying his chicken coop or bananas. He looked at me, baffled by how Ashraf and Hakimaakka were rushing towards us, by how desperate they seemed. Ibrahim folded his umbrella and shuffled ahead to meet them midway. I grabbed the end of my mundu and wrung it, waiting. I looked down towards Ashraf's house. I could see Pathumma in her flooded yard, peering at us, craning her incredibly long neck. When I turned back, Ashraf was saying something to Ibrahim and then all three of them were walking towards me, their haste unabated.

'What's the matter, Ashraf?'

'Crossed paths with some four strangers?' he said.

'What of them?'

'Well, something strange has happened, Imran. Remember the wind? Hakimaakka's mahogany crashed in the storm and I had come up to ensure he was safe in his house.'

'Cough up what you are getting at.'

'Go home, boys,' Hakimaakka was saying. 'Your mother will prefer to tell the story herself, whatever it is.'

I said to Ashraf, 'Cut short the story to a single sentence, will you?'

'Let them learn it from their mother, Ashraf,' Hakimaakka interrupted once again.

Ashraf regarded Hakimaakka and then Ibrahim and then he turned to me and continued, 'Well, so we saw it together, me and Hakimaakka. There were four men and Nabeesumma was talking to them, like something really serious, and one of them slapped her twice. Right here.'

'Slapped whom?' Ibrahim took two quick steps towards Ashraf. Hakimaakka tried to intervene again and say something but Ibrahim pushed him aside. 'Repeat what you just said.' His loud voice was even louder now with perturbation and disbelief.

'Just what you heard,' Ashraf said, 'that's what happened. One of them slapped Nabeesumma. Twice. She hit the ground. Literally. We saw it with our very own naked eyes.'

My whole being froze for a shocked second, unable to believe what I had heard let alone react. Ibrahim sprinted away home for Imma and I sprinted in the other direction, towards the Bazaar. I could hear Hakimaakka crying my name. I could hear Ibrahim crying my name even as he was running for Imma in the opposite direction. But my anger was such that I had no control over my own body and mind and my heart was racing. I couldn't let them amble away. I couldn't let them go.

Fawaz

'You didn't have to push his mother that way,' I said. Vappa said nothing. My brothers were silent too. 'She didn't do anything.'

'She just slipped I think,' Junaid said.

Vappa remained silent. We were walking back from Nabeesumma's house along the trail in single file. Our father was ahead of us, I was right behind him and behind me were my two brothers. Somehow arranged in descending order according to our age. With the oldest of us leading and the youngest trailing right behind the third. That is, Saud, our father, was leading, and Rizvan was trailing all of us, right behind Junaid.

'That's no manly thing to do, whatever the issue,' I said.

Rizvan said, 'I swear she fell on her own. She just slipped, I think.'

'My name is Saud and I do what I do,' Vappa said, 'so what's your problem? Do I owe you an explanation?'

'What do you mean?' I said.

'Did you see me push her down to make her fall?'

'Yes, I think so.'

'So what if I did?'

I could only hear his voice, not see his face. I was walking right behind him.

'That's not a manly thing to do,' I said. 'That's a mean thing to do. So out of character. You don't place your hand on a woman no matter how serious the matter. But sure you do, in fact you are used to. You are used to slapping our mother and that's the reason why she calls you Saudi Arabia.'

Junaid was chuckling. 'Saudi Arabia,' he said, and he was chuckling.

'My name is Saud and I do what I do.' I said, mimicking Vappa. Junaid chuckled louder this time, walking right behind me.

'Sure,' he said, 'but in Saudi Arabia this wouldn't have happened. Nobody would have dared to knock on the door of someone else's wife. This sure wouldn't have happened in Saudi Arabia.'

That brought us back to what we had gone there for: To give this cheeky Burhan two tight slaps on both his cheeks. So that he understood there was a price to pay for such deeds. To let him know that there would be a heavier price to pay if he were to repeat his dirty deeds. So that the dirty bastard wouldn't touch my aunt Reyhana with his dirty hands one more dirty time. But he wasn't home. We were disappointed and just walking back to our Willys, parked right in the centre of the Bazaar.

'In Saudi Arabia, for such an act, they would deprive him of his very thing that led him to her and send the woman along with him to death in a pelter of stones,' Vappa said.

'He pushed her neither strongly nor intentionally. He just wanted his way and she just slipped and fell down. That's all. So what are you quarrelling about?' Junaid said. 'We are here on business and let's think what to do next.'

Two men crossed our path. I lifted my umbrella a little for a passing glance at their faces to make sure that Burhan wasn't among them. Because they looked a lot like Burhan. At that time we didn't know they were his brothers. We didn't even know he had any brothers. We all regarded them as they gave us our way and then we walked on quietly towards the main road.

We got back in our Willys and sat in silence. The rain stopped. I was behind the wheel and Junaid said, 'Well, what do we do now?'

'I am not going anywhere without slapping the bastard's cheeks,' I said. 'I am going to sit here and wait.'

'Sure. He deserves some serious blows.' Rizvan was the only graduate in our undereducated house, so whenever he spoke everybody listened with attention. 'But is it best to meet him right at the Bazaar and let the whole of Vaiga and even the town know what our aunt is up to with a boy fifteen years her junior? Or do we just trail him quietly to his home and take up the matter in front of the family, humiliate him in front of his own family?'

'The latter is certainly not an option. Not since Vappa pushed her down,' I said.

Vappa said nothing. He was sitting right next to me, on the left. Up the slope, we could see the exodus from the mosque where everyone had been stranded in the terrible storm after the Friday prayers. They were now coming down towards the Bazaar in droves.

'Confronting him here in the very middle of the village, with all those people watching, is certainly not an option either, don't you think?' Junaid said.

'I am not going anywhere without slapping his cheeks, no matter what you say,' I said.

'What about what Rafeed said?' Vappa said. 'Didn't he message that Burhan was one of the first to leave the mosque? How can we expect to see him among the people now arriving if that's the case?'

'But he isn't home either, right?' I said.

Nobody responded. Vappa got out of the Willys to watch the crowd swarming down the slope, their sheer number, still some fair distance away. But we could see them from this far down, through our old Willys's bleary windshield.

'Anyway, I think it's impossible to spot the boy among all these people even if he were among them,' Vappa said. 'But, Good Lord, look. How big a mosque do they have here in Vaiga? I think we have come not only in the wrong weather but at the wrong time too.'

'I am not going anywhere without finishing this business today itself,' I said again.

'Let's not turn this into some movie scene,' Vappa said, settling back in his seat.

'Let's go now,' Junaid said.

'Come, start the engine,' Rizvan said.

It seemed their anger was cooling. Because they had been really angry when I told them that Rafeed had texted me that the congregation was about to get over and Burhan was at the mosque. At that time they had even wanted to kill him. Such was their anger. We had been waiting for him around the fields for six nights—ever since the rain began—and when Rafeed texted me today that Burhan was at the mosque, we couldn't wait any longer. Then, on our way to Vaiga, came another message from Rafeed—*Burhan has left the mosque.*

The first time I heard about it was some two weeks ago, when Rafeed told me about it over a drink. I was with Rafeed and Arif at a bar in Mukkam. It was there Rafeed had told me about Burhan and aunt Reyhana and I felt like slapping his face for saying something like that in front of a third person. I was embarrassed. But it turned out that none of this was news to Arif. In fact, he began to complete the story Rafeed had begun, filling in the blanks and adding details and correcting connections. That was how I found about out aunt Reyhana and Burhan. Two weeks ago. My blood was boiling with shame and rage.

They said it began some four months ago when she had gone to collect her passport at their travel agency. Rafeed and Arif had gone on a tea-break and their friend Burhan was at the counter, dealing with the customers. They said that's how Burhan and my aunt had met. Four months ago. I wondered whether they were making up the whole thing. I asked them if they were playing a prank on me. If so, I warned them, rising from my chair, you better stop now than two sentences later. But then Rafeed pointed out that my aunt had a visa issued for Umrah, that I could go to her house and find out whether the visa was used for the purpose it was issued for or not. That sat me down in my chair again. I didn't know whether aunt had applied for a permit for Umrah, but I knew that she hadn't gone to Saudi Arabia ever, certainly not in the last four months. I left for home. I asked Vappa whether there was any talk of aunt Reyhana going to Saudi Arabia to perform Umrah, any conversation that he happened to remember from the recent past.

'Yes,' he said, 'of course. But she cancelled the trip because of something I can't recall.'

Something he couldn't recall.

And that was the first time I believed there was some truth in what they had said. I did not know Burhan personally, but I had often heard them mention his name, seen a photo or two. Among other things, some three times or more they said his age

family. So I told Rafeed to keep an eye on, or arrange someone to keep an eye on, the fields. Two nights later, the night before the rain, he woke me up from sleep to say that Burhan was on his business as usual and that this time he himself was the witness. My blood boiled but I managed to fall asleep anyway. The next morning I told Vappa that Burhan was going about his business as usual. I asked him whether he intended handing out two blows to him or not.

'Sure,' he said. 'Let's hand out two blows to him. After that I intend to take it up with Reyhana.'

'So let's go now?' I said.

'I don't want the whole village to bear witness to this,' Rizvan said.

'If you do it in public, Sadique will come to know,' Vappa said. 'And that would upset him. I don't want my brother upset. He has always been a very sensitive man.'

'Let's wait for him tonight,' Rizvan said. 'Let's see whether he crosses the fields again.'

So, from the night it began to rain, for six nights we waited for him around the fields, but he didn't turn up. We all sat inside the Willys looking towards our aunt's house with a lot of hate and waited for Burhan with a lot of anger, but he didn't turn up. And by then we had run out of patience. So, when I woke up this morning, I called Rafeed, asked him if he could text me if Burhan was in attendance at their mosque for Friday prayers. He did. We were at the mosque in our own village some three kilometres away, me and my brothers and our father. I told them what the message from Rafeed said: that Burhan was present at the mosque and the congregation was about to disperse. We drove off right away without even waiting to finish the prayers. Such was our anger. Then, on the way to Vaiga, came his message that Burhan had left the mosque. I drove faster. The Bazaar wore a deserted look because it was Friday and raining. Everyone was either at home or at the mosque. Our plan was to meet Burhan at his house and hand out two long-due blows and return home without much hollering. That was the plan at the time and at the time they were all really angry, just as I was. Even Vappa. But we did not find Burhan at home and now, seated inside the Willys, their anger seemed to have cooled down. They weren't as angry as they were when Rafeed had messaged me. They were cautious now. Each of them suggested returning home, promising me that we would choose a better time today itself. I was unconvinced.

'A private disgrace is always preferable to a public disgrace,' Vappa said.

'You don't have to repeat that all the time,' I said.

'Would you rather Sadique commit suicide? Think of the disgrace it's going to bring in its wake. He shouldn't know about the developments, I think. And, besides, he has always been emotionally weak, even as a child.'

'Even you are,' I snapped.

'What am I?'

'Sentimental and weak.'

'Don't keep irritating Vappa,' Junaid said. 'Turn the engine on and let's get going.'

For a moment I watched the hundreds of people streaming down the slope, returning home from the mosque, happy about the unexpected relief from the rain.

I turned the engine on. I revved up and turned the wheel

sharply. The Willys didn't move. It seemed like the tyre was stuck. Vappa got down and picked up a flat piece of rock from the roadside and pushed it deep in the mud under the tyre and looked at me. I revved up the engine for a moment more before shifting the gear and lowering the pedal with slow intensity and swung the Willys across the road in a bumpy U-turn. But, before Vappa could get back in his seat beside me in the front, one of those guys appeared from behind the Willys, one of those two guys who had crossed our path on the trail, panting from running but not parting his lips even a sliver. He came up from behind and now he stood facing Vappa. Vappa took a step towards him and he took two steps back. Then he opened his lips.

'Did you slap my mother?' he said. 'Did you? Did you? Did you? Did you slap Nabeesu?'

'My God.' Junaid's whisper sounded like a prayer.

It seemed that things were about to get out of hand. The guy was taller than any of us and well-built. A real hulk. He looked like one in the grip of a rage beyond his control. I stirred in my seat, unsure what to do.

'What is your name, son?' Vappa said.

'My name is Imran, and I am Nabeesu's second,' he said. 'I asked you whether you slapped my mother or not. I asked if I heard that right.' He was very loud. The whole village could have heard him. In the rear-view mirror I could see the returnees from the mosque approach the Bazaar.

'No, I didn't. But listen,' Vappa said, 'listen, my son.' Vappa took two steps towards him and he retreated two steps.

My left hand clutched the trembling knob of the gear lever. My right hand was on the steering wheel, my fingers tapping nervously. Rizvan and Junaid got out of the Willys and flanked Vappa, two steps behind him. They moved closer to Imran and Imran took a few steps backwards and now they all stood right in front of the bonnet. I was watching it all through the windshield as it happened and it all happened in a blink.

'Listen, my son,' Vappa was saying.

Imran stood facing the Willys, his hands behind his waist.

'Listen.'

Imran released his right hand from behind his back, took two quick steps towards my father and struck the right side of his face with a stone bigger than his hand could hold and, before I could believe what was happening, before even Rizvan and Junaid could react despite standing so near, Imran sent the same stone hurtling at the windshield with a long scream and I swerved and lowered myself in my seat, holding my hands over my head. The stone cracked the windshield and dropped on the bonnet with a heavy thud and rolled down.

Chinnan

I told Shahid about Burhan because of my inability to keep a secret. It's an instinct I can't shed, no matter how hard I try. I knew that Panchami would scold me when I told her what I had told Shahid. Using words like irresponsibility and consequence. But I had an itch to tell him and that's my instinct and I could do nothing about it. Instincts cannot be tamed by social education. I told Shahid what I told Shahid because I had no choice. I harboured no personal dislike for Burhan just as I felt no special liking for Shahid. So, when he told me to spread the news, I said that wasn't my business. But he seemed not to have heard because the only response was the beep signalling that the call was over.

Informing someone—anyone aside from Panchami—was enough to satisfy my itch. Then the urge would be appeased.

It's always been my curse, this inability to keep a secret. All I can say is that things have happened in the past because of my tongue. I had told people things I shouldn't have in the past and things had happened, it was true, but what was also true was that secret things had a way of seeking a witness in me. Just like Burhan sought witness in me a few days ago as he crossed the paddy fields with a flashlight when it hadn't yet rained and the night was clear and awash with stars.

I was out fishing that night, just as I was out fishing today. And that night I had studied the progress of his flashlight until it had ceased flashing around Reyhana's house. I had told this to Shahid the next day because Shahid was the first one I came across the next morning. I was out brushing my teeth when he passed by on the trail along with two women. He came down the moment he saw me, leaving the women behind. He said they were going from home to home on the state government's measles-rubella inoculation sensitisation drive.

Panchami brought us tea and we talked party things. We belonged to the same political party, Shahid and I—the communist party. That's when the terrible itch began to kick in. So I leant across and told him in a hushed voice what I had seen. It soon piqued his interest and he was asking more questions, questions I had no answers for because I had seen Burhan only once and knew nothing more than what I had seen. But before he left, Shahid told me to inform him if I happened to see Burhan again, saying he himself intended to keep an eye out. I said nothing. I wasn't interested in extreme responses to my divulgences. Not that I have any power over it, but I wasn't interested in extreme reactions, like Shahid's, who looked really upset. As if it were his, not Sadique's, wife, that Burhan was screwing. Panchami was upset too. When I told her that I told Shahid what I had seen, she did not talk to me for three days, and whenever I tried to mollify her, she raised hell about every small non-issue. She never approved of this trait of mine, of making news out of secrets and gossiping in general. What business is it of yours, she would hiss in anger. She is a straightforward woman who doesn't want to trespass on what's others' business, even as a passive listener. For three days I spent my time at home, telling her that I regretted telling Shahid what I had seen. I told her I would not tell Shahid if I happened to see Burhan ever again. And I told her that I hoped never to see Burhan again, doing what he was doing. But the problem was that I saw Burhan doing what he was doing once again, this time during the day, and I couldn't resist the itch, I tried hard but I just couldn't.

Today it was my son's turn to witness. But I would have seen him anyway because that's my fate. He pointed to Burhan and I stood looking at the man in the storm for what seemed like a long time, almost five minutes, before I turned and began to walk back home with my son and the banded snakehead. For some time, I resisted the itch successfully, and then I couldn't. I phoned Shahid and told him what I had seen: Burhan and Reyhana. The news seemed to have set fire to his nether regions. He began to rant about morality and culture and the Gulf and the desert sun and husbands and the holiness of fucking one's husband alone. Stuff like that. I said nothing. I just listened until he asked me to spread the news. When he said that, I told him that's not my business, but he disconnected the call. I was a bit surprised by the fervour with which he was carrying on, speaking words raw with violence, as if, like I said before, it were his wife and not Sadique's that Burhan was screwing. So I carried on homewards with my son and the snakehead. By the time I reached home, the rain had ceased miraculously.

I told Panchami what I had told Shahid. It would have been pointless trying to hide it from her. Sometimes I think my only problem is that I am too truthful and my special misfortune is that too many things are revealed to me, things others are not privy to. Call it the Chinnan Paradox. I told Panchami that I saw Burhan once again on his way to the house of his mistress and that I had told Shahid about it once again. She was silent, looking at me. So I told her without looking at her that Shahid sounded a bit wild about the whole thing, asking me to call up people and all. Only when I said it did I discover the existence of such an apprehension in me. And suddenly it sounded like a more serious scenario than I had imagined and the worst scenario I had imagined was divorce for Reyhana. I hadn't imagined any other scenario maybe because I didn't like to imagine extreme consequences for my divulgences. But the discovery of my apprehension, the apprehension that Shahid might raise a mob, threatened even my peace.

I looked at her, waiting for the anger to surface on her face.

Panchami collected the fish from my hand and put it on the table, rubbed her hands together, raised her right hand in the air like some WWF wrestlers on TV do, and slapped me on my right cheek.

She cried, 'I have told you a hundred times not to bother with what isn't your business, haven't I?' She was hissing, seething with anger. I could hear the gnashing of her teeth. Her lips were trembling like a stutterer's, her whole body was convulsing. 'Two women have been divorced because of you and you aren't yet finished with your eavesdropping and seeing things and passing on news.'

Only when she finished speaking did I realise that I had been slapped. I could feel the vibrant buzz of the slap pass from my right ear to my left ear like electricity. And then I could feel the pain. Of both the slap and the humiliation of the slap because I had been slapped by my wife in front of my own son: this had no precedence in our family book. But I neither had the strength to slap her back—she was taller than me, 5′11″ something, and stronger, with big hands and broad man-shoulders—nor felt it morally right to quarrel or offer justifications because what she said was true. The humiliation was deep and the resentment would stay for long. With the slap I forgot all about Burhan. I just walked into the room without looking at her or the child and shut the door on her. I decided that I wouldn't open the door or eat at home until she apologised.

At noon we were busy loving, happy about the rain and its pleasant cold. But now we were unhappy again. I dragged the chair and opened the window. A breeze grazed my face. I couldn't believe it wasn't raining any more. I opened my bottle of rum and poured a drink. The power went off again.

It seemed that Panchami wasn't finished slapping me yet. She banged on the door until I opened it. Her eyes were blazing with fury. I went back to my chair again and sat down, looking out of the window, drinking rum neat.

'The only problem is that I can't help but tell you whatever I have done,' I said.

'What does that even mean?' she said.

'If I didn't tell you that I told Shahid what I saw, there wouldn't have been any problem at all.'

'How?' she wanted to know.

'Well, if I didn't tell you that I told Shahid, you wouldn't know anything about it at all. So your knowing is the problem.'

'So you mean, I can let a Burhan in when you are out, and unless you know anything about it, there isn't any problem in it at all?'

'That isn't what I meant. I was only explaining my helplessness. I happen to see and hear things and I happen to disclose them. I am incapable of hiding—from you in particular.'

'No. If it were helplessness, if it was just about wanting to tell someone what you have seen or heard to deal with an inborn itch, you might have come and told me this in the first place, not Shahid. Not that I would have enjoyed hearing about what others were doing with their genitals, but I would have made an effort to put myself through it all if, by telling me, your itch would cease itching and the secret would end its painful life inside you. But NO. Instead, as usual, you come to tell me that you have seen something and shared the story with someone. So it's not helplessness. Only a few days ago, when you told me what you told Shahid about Burhan, I told you not to fuck up others' lives any more. You choose to see things, you choose to hear things and then you tell things where you want to tell because it excites you to see others in misery. You intentionally foment trouble in others' lives. Deceiving yourself with false excuses, not wanting to admit to your character, blaming it all on some juvenile tactlessness.'

'Well, you are more eloquent than you need to be, I would say,' I said.

'I am not done slapping you yet,' she almost screamed. 'You have caused at least two divorces. As far as I know, that is. At least half a dozen land disputes were the result of your seeing and eavesdropping and telling things to people, one of which ended in a stabbing spree, remember? All the youth in this village know that it's you who spoils their marriage prospects by talking ill of their habits and character to the men from the girls' side. Isn't that the reason they call you Djinn here? With one year of membership, you tore the local committee members of the communist party into three different factions, they say. And whom have you chosen as the moral leader to confess your dirty secret to? Shahid. One whose wife ditched him for a mullah. Now don't feign innocence. You chose him, you sought him out because you knew he was going to take it personally.'

I could hear the distant brawl at the Bazaar. It seemed to distract even Panchami. Even Damu, who stood by her in a fresh T-shirt and shorts. I wondered what it was about and wanted to go to the Bazaar to find out right away. Once again I was all impulse. I stood up to go but my wife slapped me again, this time on my left cheek with the back of her right hand. The slap sat me down. The longer I looked at her the more she seemed determined to slap me if I uttered another word in my defence. So I said nothing more, even though humiliation was flaring inside me.

This was the second slap in front of my son. I looked at my son.

Panchami grabbed my phone from the table and dragged Damu with her as she bolted out of the room and latched the door from the outside. I ran towards the window. Let me out, I cried, but there was no answer. She was in the front yard, looking out. I looked with her. Men from different houses were scampering towards the Bazaar. The entire neighbourhood was astir. I banged the window harder and harder and screamed my apologies to Panchami, who was still out there, scanning the neighbourhood, with my phone in her hand. Open the door, I cried one more time. She turned to look at me once before going away, dragging our son along.

Pathumma

I could see it all, standing right there in the yard, knee-deep in water, and I could see that a big drama was unfolding on this Friday afternoon. I was puzzled and couldn't understand what all the trouble was about. Why would anyone want to slap Nabeesumma? I turned back and looked. June was at the door. I turned around again and looked towards the trail. I saw Ibrahim. He was running, just as his brother had run a few minutes ago, towards the Bazaar. Like a charging boar. And Ashraf was rushing too, right behind him, and I called out to him.

'Ashrafffff Ashrafffff.'

He turned his head midstride in answer and his mundu unfolded and he tripped or slipped and went rolling down the trail. But he was quick to get back on his feet and, as if nothing had happened, as if he hadn't heard my voice, as if he couldn't care less even if he had heard my voice, hobbled away towards the Bazaar.

'Ashraffff Ashraffff.'

But he was gone. Just like the others before him. Imran, Hakimaakka and Ibrahim. I could already hear the brawl at the Bazaar. I waded across the yard and went up the steep and stood looking over the whole place, this neighbourhood on the terraced terrain, waking from six days of relentless rain to a surprise Friday brawl. Women were already outside their houses, whispering to each other in hushed voices, and men were leaping over each other's fences, hurrying in different directions on a dozen trails. Soon enough the whole neighbourhood had turned into a commotion.

June was now standing on the porch, looking down at the swirling water.

'Go inside and shut the door,' I cried as loud as I could.

She didn't so much as lift her head. She just stood still, lifeless, like a statue of June. My strange June. My twelve-year-old June. Our problem girl. I have never understood whether she was precocious or just mental like her father's dead mother. I stared at her until she went inside the house and shut the door.

Ramlatha, Hakimaakka's wife, and Panchami along with her son joined me on the trail. Our neighbour Roshan came along, panting, and I stopped him. We all looked at each other. Roshan was, needless to say, in a hurry. I had to hold his arm to stop him. But, before I could ask him what was going on, he asked me what was going on at the Bazaar. So I told him my part of the story: the four strangers, Nabeesumma, the slap (two slaps), Ashraf and Hakimaakka, Imran and Ibrahim, the fight. I also told him about Burhan because it was Burhan they came looking for, because it was Burhan's house they asked me for.

'Slapped Nabeesumma?' Panchami snapped, not ready to believe it at all. 'Who?'

They all looked surprised, even Panchami's morose-looking child, that frog-eyed Damu, my weird June's weirder classmate.

Roshan looked up from his phone while continuing to type on WhatsApp. 'Well, they are Saud, Sadique's brother, and his sons. Chinnan saw Burhan on his way to Reyhana's house earlier. The news has been viral on WhatsApp for a few minutes now.' He looked at Panchami, as though afraid of what she might say.

Panchami said nothing.

'Why did they slap Nabeesu?' Ramlatha said.

'They came looking for Burhan,' I said.

'What did Chinnan say?' Panchami wanted to know.

'My God, Burhan and Reyhana?' I couldn't believe what I heard. 'That's almost a twenty-year difference, I would say.'

'That's plain wrong,' Ramlatha said. 'Gross. You don't slap a mother for a son's wrongdoing.'

'Did Chinnan say that to you?' Panchami repeated her question to Roshan. Roshan was desperate to go and in no mood to complete the story for Panchami, but she grabbed his other arm. That finally made him look up from his phone.

'It's all on WhatsApp already, circulating in a dozen groups. Check your phones.' And then he shook himself free of her grip and hurried on towards the Bazaar, typing typing typing.

The brawl was getting louder and louder. People were rushing past us. I could see them scampering down sloping terraces, hopping fences, scrambling towards the Bazaar. The gloomiest, most ordinary day had suddenly become extraordinary. It hadn't even been ten minutes since they started fighting and the quietest day had already become utter chaos.

'Achchan saw,' Damu said. 'Even I saw.'

'What did you see?' Ramlatha stooped to hear the boy.

'We saw Burhanikka going across the fields,' Damu said.

Panchami spanked her boy on the butt with her phone. 'Can't you keep your mouth shut?' she snarled. 'Can't you and your father keep your mouth shut?' She gave the boy one gentle slap on the face and turned to Ramlatha. 'What are you stooping for? That's a boy only twelve years old. Aren't you ashamed of extracting sleazy details from a boy forty years your junior?'

That straightened Ramlatha's back. 'But if the story is true, then it's gross. But what I can't understand is why Nabeesu was slapped. What purpose did that serve? Could it un-fuck Reyhana? Un-birth Burhan? What?'

Panchami looked really pissed off. With her husband, son, Roshan and now Ramlatha. 'Why don't you go and ask Nabeesumma herself,' she shouted, and with that Ramlatha shuffled away towards the Bazaar in the company of other women.

'Did they really slap Nabeesumma?' Panchami wondered.

'Why?' I said. 'That's what Ashraf said. Ashraf and Hakimaakka.'

'Do you think we should go and check on her? To see how she's doing.'

I could see June on the porch again, gazing at us. 'Who?'

'Nabeesumma.'

'Oh, better not, I would say,' I said. 'She won't appreciate it. She isn't the type.'

We could hear the brawl at the Bazaar. It was unlike anything I could remember. Getting louder and louder all the time.

'Do you want to go and see what's happening there instead?'

'Where? To see what?' she said. 'To the Bazaar? No. Do you have Burhan's number?'

'Why? I must have it on my phone and my phone is in my room.'

'Don't you think the boy is in trouble if he is still there?'

That's when I realised that the story of Reyhana and Burhan was true. 'You think so?'

'Let's go down and get your phone.'

'If he is there with her, then there will be trouble,' I said. 'But if the news has been passed around on WhatsApp as Roshan says, then either he must know it already, or Nabeesumma or one of his brothers or anyone from around here who knows him would have called him by now and he must have fled. But even if he's not there with her now, there will be trouble later for sure. But you can try his number anyway.'

Only after saying that did unease dawn on me and I became a little unsure. Ashraf was not going to like it. To have Panchami and her son inside our house. But I reckoned that Ashraf wasn't going to come back from the Bazaar any time soon. Panchami looked at me and said nothing. Her child was glowering at her with his frog-eyes, holding her hand. We went down towards my home, where June was standing on the porch, waving at Damu, her classmate and friend.

Nabeesumma

Then the rain hushed. The wind hushed. Like God willed it and it hushed. Like God caught the wind by its throat and it hushed. Like that and it was all gone.

It was kind of quiet then, even though the trees dripped heavily and the roof still leaked steadily from all its thirty dirty holes. Yes, I could hear the watery noise all around the house, yet my ears were quiet somehow. What wasn't quiet was my mind and my mind was on a trip of its own. Peaceless in delirium.

Imran never took his phone to the mosque and that's how I could keep trying to call Burhan because I have never had a phone. But Burhan's phone was switched off. I tried Ahmad and Ahmad was out of reach. Dulqar and Rashid weren't picking up. Ibrahim had forgotten his phone because, when I tried his number, it began to ring and vibrate from somewhere in the toilet.

I knew they weren't going to kill my youngest as they had threatened to do, but I didn't want them to so much as lay their hands on him. I knew they weren't going to kill my son, I believed. Sure, I was upset with my son. My worry for him was subdued only by the shame of what he had done or what they accused him of doing. I just wished I could whip the shame of it out of him just as I used to when he was a child. Each time I thought about Reyhana's age, a little blast of humiliation coughed out of me. I hated her as well. I hated Reyhana's shameless audacity to lure a boy at least fifteen years her junior. If nothing else, at forty, she should have been able to reckon with the consequences. But, then, Reyhana didn't have a face. I had never seen her. I had seen her husband, Sadique, but not his wife, this Reyhana. So I hated a faceless Reyhana. I hated her audacity and I hated her criminal indifference to consequences. But I hated my son more. At twenty-five, sex wasn't such an unbearable lack to have driven him to seek it with a woman only nine years younger than me. I hated him for putting Nabeesu through such humiliation, such dishonour. Because that's all Nabeesu had to take to her grave: honour. Because Nabeesu had begged nobody for anything, owed nobody a paisa, nor had she sold her body to feed the Ox and his five Bulls in the house. Nabeesu had held her neck upright, stooping before nobody but God, only to plead to that Eternal Troublemaker to take a nap from troubling Nabeesu so much. Nabeesu hadn't gone seeking men either even though that would have been fair and blameless because Nabeesu hadn't seen a man naked, including her husband, for the past twenty-five years. But Nabeesu had emerged unscathed from all the troubles God had ever laid down in her path till this day.

I hated my son because he was out blemishing my honour, the family's honour, and I hated him all the more because he could have helped it. At twenty-five he could have helped himself out of the situation even if at forty Reyhana couldn't. And I hated him for keeping his phone switched off. I wanted to warn him about the situation, I wanted to tell him to be careful not to bump into them on the way home. Not that I believed they would kill him, but I didn't want them to even touch my son. And, besides, men were rash and reckless and unpredictable animals capable of actions with irreversible consequences. So I kept dialling Burhan and Rashid and Dulqar.

That man pushed me out of his way and I slipped and fell,

butt down, in the puddle of mud. That's what had happened.

My nightie was wet and smeared with dirt. I could feel my wet hair on my wet back, daubs of dirt behind my neck. My hips hurt and my forehead hurt, surprised by the fall. I put down the phone and held a pocket mirror to my face. The cut on my forehead was bigger than I had felt it to be and it was bleeding a little still. What had caused that cut? I couldn't remember hitting my head during the fall. I went to the kitchen to seal the cut because I wanted none of my children to see it. I coiled some cobweb round my finger, rubbed it in my palm, and stuck it on the cut. I held the mirror to my face again, but the cut was still visible.

I heard Hakimaakka crying, Imraaan Imraaan. Ibrahim crying, Imraaan Imraaan. When I heard their voices screaming for Imran, I knew that the situation was not anymore in my control. I opened the door because Ibrahim was banging on it. Before he could say anything at all, I cried, 'Go get Burhan.'

To my dismay, he asked me whether I had been slapped and by whom and for what. I denied that anybody had slapped me and cut him short every time he opened his mouth, saying, 'Hush now and go get Burhan. Don't let him run into the hands of those people.' Ibrahim stood looking at all the dirt in my wet nightie. He stood looking at the cut on my forehead. And then he opened the door and he was gone. Ashraf was standing outside the house, waiting for Ibrahim.

'Where is Imran?'

I also wanted to ask him who had told Ibrahim and Imran that I had been slapped because I couldn't think of anyone who could have told my sons that. But I couldn't because he, too, had gone off like an excited dog after Ibrahim.

Imran's phone rang. It was Nishiya, my sister. I picked up the call and she asked me what was going on.

'Where is Burhan?'

'Why?' I said. 'What happened?'

'They say he is with Reyhana, Sadique's wife. Right now, they say.'

My heart skipped two beats. 'How do you know?'

'How do I know? Everybody knows. Send one of the boys, I say. Send one of the boys and get him out if it's true that he's there with her because they are going to beat him dead.'

'How do you know?'

'Dig him out. Send one of your boys because Burhan's phone is switched off.'

'How do you know?'

'Do I know what, Nabeesu, do I know what?' She was shouting now, my polite sister.

'That Burhan is with Reyhana at this moment? That his phone is switched off? How do you know all this?'

'I called him. That's how. Everybody knows, Nabeesu. Everybody knows. The whole of Vaiga and beyond Vaiga and beyond the river and even in faraway Arabia people know.'

'How do they know?'

'Please check WhatsApp on Imran's phone, Nabeesu, please,' she cried.

I cut Nishiya's call because Dulqar, my third useless son, was calling. I asked him if he knew where Burhan was. He said he didn't. I asked him where he was at the moment. He said Rashid and he were walking back home from the mosque.

Dulqar seemed unaware of all that was happening. He didn't

even seem to know that his brothers had picked up a fight at the Bazaar with the people who had come looking for Burhan. I could hear the clamour of the fight. Announcing to the whole village the great dishonour that Burhan had brought upon Nabeesu's house. Dulqar also seemed to be unaware of what Nishiya said was happening on WhatsApp.

The mosque stood a good half mile up the slope from the Bazaar. I imagined they had got late and were just beginning to leave the mosque. The noisy fight at the Bazaar may not be audible that far up. I didn't want them to run into the fight as well. I wanted to dissuade them or divert them from running into the others, so that one of them at least could go and dig Burhan out of Reyhana's room and save him from the beating if indeed the rumours had it right. So I told him what Nishiya told me: about Burhan and Reyhana. About WhatsApp. I also told him that Burhan's phone was switched off. His lack of surprise at my breathless revelation told me that he knew what I was talking about, that he was feigning ignorance so as to not set ablaze my smouldering head. He told me not to worry, that he would let no one harm Burhan.

I could hear him whisper to someone, Rashid maybe.

'Who are you whispering to?'

Dulqar didn't answer. I could hear them whispering. Then he cut the call. I kept dialling his number over and over, but he didn't pick up. I couldn't guess what had transpired, why he had to cut the call, but I knew he was talking to Rashid. I knew that the younger brothers had gone to join their older brothers in the fight.

All this was happening too quickly for me to fully realise what was happening. I just couldn't absorb the shock of it all. The sheer confusion of it all. So, now what? Now what? My four sons were fighting four men in the middle of the Bazaar to avenge a slap I never received. A vengeance I never sought. Now what? The honour of the family was in peril. My head was exploding with concern for Burhan and Burhan's phone was still switched off. I didn't know what to do next. I could hear the excitement of the fight on the street. I could hear people outside, rushing towards the Bazaar, happily panicking.

Allah, I said. My thoughts had trespassed and my tongue had sinned, I admit to it, but be kind in your punishments. Allah, I beseeched, have mercy on this small old sinner and be kind in your punishments. My misery and I are here to stay long enough to atone for all my sins, so be kind in your punishments. I sat down on my bed in a kind of silent prayer.

The world was quieter except for an occasional thunder and the dripping trees, shaken by the slow intermittent wind. Through the window lightning shone in soundless phosphorescence. In the blue of burning plastic. A spider moved slowly up the stile of the old rusted window and glided away across the grill, weaving its silk along. On the stool of the window a butterfly had slept into sound decay in a powder of wings. On the wall above, a lizard that had been asleep for a week now sprinted up, as if scared by its own sudden waking, and hid behind the clock. And the clock ticked heavily, just like my heart.

Now what? I had no answer to that question.

Ashraf

I sprained my ankle by tripping on my mundu and falling while running after Ibrahim. The sprained ankle slowed my pace. The fall was bad and even the excitement of all that was unfolding did nothing to prevent the ankle from swelling. I fought the pain and went on to the Bazaar. On the way, I had to share my part of the story with a few men and even women, and some of them shared with me what was happening on WhatsApp: Burhan and Reyhana, of which, until then, I knew nothing. By the time I reached the Bazaar, I was limping like a cripple, jostled around by people. By the time I reached the Bazaar, the whole world knew who the four men were: Saud and his sons.

When I reached, Dulqar and Rashid—Burhan's other two brothers—were just arriving at the scene. I pushed my way forward blindly until I was right behind the two of them, managing to ignore the pain of my ankle for one excited moment. When I could see again, I was at the centre of a bloody rage. Imran had two of Saud's sons under each arm and Ibrahim was rolling on the tarmac, rolling and getting kicked and punched on the head by Saud whose white-bearded face and whiter hair were a mess of blood. Saud, bending low, was punching Ibrahim in his face and sides and the back of his head while the other son kicked him on the butt and stomach and the crowd spread backwards making space in hurried negotiation.

I was stunned and panting.

But I couldn't stay still. Nobody could stay still. I saw Dulqar slap a phone out of one boy's hand, but that wasn't enough.

There were too many boys with too many phones shooting the fight, with hands high up in the air, pushing and pulling each other for a better view.

I asked someone for the names of Saud's three sons and someone else told me, pointing each one out. I studied them until I could name them all: Fawaz, Junaid and Rizvan.

Imran still held Fawaz and Junaid by their necks under his arms and he was hard as a rock even though the others were elbowing his stomach pretty hard. Imran needed no help from his brothers, not yet. I watched Dulqar as he moved with Rashid, confused about where to begin helping their brothers. His eyes settled on Rizvan, Saud's youngest, who was kicking and punching Ibrahim with his father. I thought Dulqar was going to jump to Ibrahim's rescue, but he couldn't. Rizvan now armed himself with a jagged stone and took two steps towards Imran from behind and drew the hand with the stone high in the air so as to crack open Imran's skull.

A gasp of panic and disbelief escaped from the crowd and hushed.

But the hand didn't deliver that fatal blow. Rashid leapt into action, landing an immense blow at Rizvan's nape and Rizvan staggered to the left like a stunned monkey and swagged along the edge of the road, the stone slipping loose from his grip into the rushing water of the overflowing gutter. But Imran, who tried to turn around to see what was going on behind him, allowed his grip on Fawaz and Junaid to loosen and in that moment they wrestled out of Imran's grip, hooked his knees with their elbows, pulled him up into the air with a cry and tossed him into the crowd.

Dulqar finally swooped into action, unleashing a series of

blows on Junaid, leaving Fawaz for Imran to handle. Junaid stooped and hunkered down, cupping his skull. Dulqar kicked him down and turned to help Ibrahim. But Ibrahim was on his feet already, reenergised by his brothers' arrival, holding Saud by his neck and pummelling him on the head.

All around me I could hear the dull sounds of their kicks and punches and slaps, their hysterical screams of pain and fury. Rashid lifted Rizvan off the ground by the scruff of his shirt and headbutted him with a brute force and he staggered backwards like a drunk on a moving surface and collapsed where he had been picked up from.

Imran stomped across to the old man in Ibrahim's grip and snarled, 'What did you slap my mother for? Who among you hasn't been suckled on mother's milk to not know where that would hurt?' He downed Saud with a single fist-blow on the top of his skull. But Saud, despite the oldness of his Santa Claus-beard and the severities of the blows he had received, got up as if he had springs for a spine. His other son, Junaid, whom Dulqar had lowered to the ground in a shower of blows just a minute ago, also got up. With an immense yell, Fawaz, whom Imran had left behind, jumped at Dulqar from behind, landing his knee on his quarry's lower back, sending him into the crowd. The next moment, Rizvan was also up and, with Fawaz, Junaid and their old man, he unleashed a furious rain of fist-blows. Three of Dulqar's brothers, at first taken aback by the newfound strength with which the four of them were attacking, now retaliated, blow for blow, in a blind and rapid exchange. The crowd roared and hushed and then for a moment you heard nothing but the steady exchange of blows.

Dulqar swung himself out of the crowd and went around the warring pack and downed Junaid and Fawaz with two blows each on the back of their heads. He was about to throw a punch at Saud as well but, in the nick of time, Rizvan kicked him straight in the crotch and Dulqar screamed in pain, his face contorting like a baby with a bitter pill in its mouth. He fell to his knees, clenching his teeth and fists. For a moment, everyone stopped to watch him in his pain. Everyone except Imran, who stomped frantically towards the Willys. He entered it from the left and came out through the right with an immense jack in hand.

That's when the crowd began to unravel. All around us people were dispersing in loud commotion, utter chaos. It confused me just as it confused all the fighters because I was just as involved in the fight as the fighters themselves. I knew a lot was going on around me, all about Burhan and Reyhana, but I just hadn't realised the gravity of what was cooking. The fighters, who even a moment earlier looked unstoppable, now froze in the unanticipated mayhem, this unscripted chaos, looking incomprehensibly befuddled. The jack slipped loose from Imran's grip. Someone stepped on my sprained ankle and I spun on the other leg, squirming with pain, and even before I could scurry to safety from the stampede, I was pushed and I stumbled on one leg and fell into the gutter. By the time I emerged again, all of Nabeesumma's sons were gone. By the time I was up on my feet again, three quarters of the crowd was gone.

'What a day,' somebody exclaimed.

I crawled out of the gutter and dragged myself on one leg down the road, towards the fields.

Imam Shahnavaz

I hated the time I had to spend there. I hated it. But I had to bear it because each household under the jurisdiction of the mosque was bound to host me for a week. That's how the mosque committee has been covering my food expenses ever since I was made the Imam here and I have been Imam here for three decades. It meant that I wouldn't repeat a household for six months, and the cycle would only get longer because the number of houses under the mosque was increasing. But, over the years, every third house was somehow unhappy about my visits and it was evident in their reception when I appeared at their doors without a choice, with an awkward helpless smile of apology on my face.

That wasn't the case earlier, let's say some twenty years ago, or even ten–fifteen years ago when the electronic age hadn't quite arrived. In those days I didn't feel like an intruder when they opened their doors for me three times a day. They had welcoming faces, wished me salaam three times a day. But even in those days, Shahid's parents were a case apart. They have always intensely disliked having me over at their lunches and dinners. And they let me know that with words and with eyes. Even though Shahid's mother cooked better than any other lady in the village, I could never enjoy eating there because they made me feel like an unwelcome necessity, an embarrassing relic straight from the medieval times. So, today I had decided to say a thing or two about the rain to Shahid's father, eat quickly and rush back to the mosque for a long siesta. We said a thing or two about the weather and, just as I was beginning to eat, they spoke of their discomfort at my presence in words I have long grown familiar with and I just couldn't eat and I hated being there.

Shahid's father was beginning to say something more, but Shahid shut them up. I began to eat quickly and silently to get it over with so I could return to the mosque where I could lie down in my room in peace for a cool siesta. Or else idle over a coffee with old jobless folks at the mosque and discuss the rain, about 1991 maybe. Shahid's mother cooked really well, especially the gooseberry-sardine. But each moment I spent in that house, with my hostile hosts gawking, was too burdensome for me to enjoy eating. I just wanted to finish the lunch and ate in haste.

Shahid's phone rang. He answered it and was silent for a moment, listening. Then we heard him shout, saying all sorts of things. I could piece together a tale of adultery just from the words he spoke. He was very angry about it. Hysterical. There was someone in the Gulf, someone he knew, whose wife was cheating on him with a man probably younger than her. A usual story made unusual because of their age-difference. Shahid's temper was rising with each breath. I watched him. He cut the call and went on a calling spree, moving restlessly about the dining room, speaking with so much aggression, with so much hostility, and that was how I learnt the names of the protagonists: Burhan, Nabeesu's youngest, and Reyhana, wife of Sadique, whose house stood across the paddy fields.

I finished my lunch, washed my hands and sat down, watching Shahid in his anger.

I continued to listen to Shahid for a few more minutes, quiet and quite confused, hoping that he might cut the call and talk to me. But Shahid went from one call to another, repeating the tale. I began to realise that he was instigating a mob. He was directing men towards Reyhana's house, he was exhorting them to kill the son of a bitch. No, he didn't say the word kill, but that was what he was rooting for. The bitch was Nabeesu and the son was Burhan. I bolted from my chair. It would have been useless spending my time arguing with Shahid. He was one impossible fellow. Truculent and full of certitudes and cocksure. Wounded by his own wife two years ago. Righteous beyond religion. Muslim beyond Islam. Shahid continued his phone calls, his parents continued watching him in a kind of dazed and restrained panic. They said nothing even as I opened the door and cleared out of the house.

Outside it wasn't raining any more, but the day was no less dark. The threat of storm still loomed low in the air and lingered in the trees. From the drainpipes on the rooftop rainwater gushed down in long arcs. I stepped out on to the road, fixing my wet turban back on my head. Where I stood, water flowed ankle-deep, and the gutters on both sides of the road were overflowing.

I was very worried as I recalled again and again the anger in Shahid's crazed voice, frenziedly calling up his friends to instigate a mob to lynch Burhan. I wanted to alert Burhan to this danger because Shahid was determined to stir up a mob and he was quite capable of raising one. But I had left my phone at the mosque, in my room, because of the rain.

The mosque was some distance down the slope still, so I walked faster. There was sudden traffic, especially of motorcycles, on the road. There were people whose house lay north but who were now scrambling south, towards the Bazaar, and I was perplexed. But I didn't stop them and inquire.

I walked faster and faster towards the mosque. The muezzin was restlessly pacing in the yard. I went up in a trot.

'Why is everyone rushing towards the Bazaar, Saida? What is going on down there?'

'Oh, you don't know yet? I thought you already knew.'

'What?'

'It's been going on for some ten minutes now.'

'Tell me what.'

Saida stopped pacing. He was excited to tell me what was going on at the Bazaar. 'That's Nabeesu's sons fighting Sadique's brother and nephews.'

'Sadique's brother and nephews?' I cried, unable to comprehend.

'It has got something to do with Sadique's wife. At least that's what I hear. Burhan's four brothers are fighting Reyhana's brother-in-law and his sons.'

'How do you know it is so?'

'WhatsApp. It's all there.'

'Unbelievable.'

'Isn't it?' he said. 'But the unbelievable will get even more unbelievable if you hear more of what's circulating on WhatsApp.'

'Tell me more of what's circulating on WhatsApp,' I said, snatching his phone from his hand and scrolling down the WhatsApp chats.

'That Burhan's screwing Reyhana right at this moment and both of their phones are switched off.'

'I see,' I said, even though I already knew that bit from Shahid. I scrolled through some WhatsApp groups to grasp the mood of the village. I returned Saida's phone, scowling. 'I see.'

Instead of going back to my room, I turned back and began to jog towards the Bazaar. I forgot my phone again. In the distance I could hear the brawl and people were streaming down the road. I stopped a motorcycle and rode pillion.

At the Bazaar the eight of them were fighting like monkeys under the carob tree, Saud and his sons and Burhan's four brothers, and the spectators stood in a ring, some far too bewildered to intervene and others far too enraptured to want to broker peace. But the fighters themselves looked uncontrollable. Kicking and swinging at each other and rolling on and off the tarmac, pummelling in violent embraces, wrestling in and out of the tangles of their twisted limbs, falling down and rising up again, headbutting, ripping each other's clothes. It looked ridiculous. Eight bearded men, each as tall as the other, were fighting. Missing fists and landing blows. Wallowing in the overflowing gutters like hippos. Brown with dirt. The fighters were constantly moving down the slope and the onlookers were moving along with them, rearranging their positions. But I couldn't move for a moment and in that moment I was outside the ring again.

A brief wind passed, shaking the carob tree. It felt like an artificial rain.

I could only hear them now, not see them. The crowd went *woooooh* and a lonely voice shouted at the top of his shrill voice to stop this madness. One of the fighters was screaming, in pain or anger I couldn't tell. The crowd danced backwards and drifted apart in chaos and then rearranged themselves in ripples around the fighters as before.

This was the most remarkable thing about this fight: nobody was intervening, nobody was trying to stop the madness. I tried in my own small way but was sucked away by the crowd. The scene was too big for this old man to handle. The crowd's refusal to intervene was unusual because usually people broke up fights. Instead, they seemed to be cheering, wildly ecstatic, their hands thrown up in the air, recording videos and uploading them on WhatsApp.

All around me I could hear the sounds of footwear, water. splashing, men and children running crazily. The crowd grew thicker and thicker until I couldn't see anything but people. They leapt up the gravel-piles and walls and wet trees and electric posts and some had even mounted the Willys. The roofs of shops and the balconies of the party offices of the communists and the Congress and the Muslim League were crammed with spectators. The banners that Copa America and Euro Cup fans had strung across the road fluttered above the fighters, Brazil and Argentina, Germany and Portugal and France. A boy climbed like a frog up the swaying flagpole of the Argentina fans. In the brief cool gusts that shook the carob tree, it rained a little again, and a giant flex board of the Brazilian national team—which the crazy wind had earlier flung to the lower branches—now slipped loose and flopped into the gutter. I stood watching it all, a confused old man.

Someone told me all this had to do with Burhan, that Burhan was at Reyhana's house. And then another told me the same story, and then another. In more or less the same words. They all had phones in their hands. Talking, recording the fight, or typing. A pandemonium of around five hundred men. And then another told me the same story. Then another. Burhan and Reyhana. RIGHT NOW, they said. Forty-five and twenty-five, they said. Twenty-five and fifty, they said. Twenty-three and forty-eight, they said. The whole Bazaar was afire with hot rumours, vitriolic with violent opinions, and all the outrageous stories of Burhan and Reyhana that seemed to lend their anger a kind of raw legitimacy.

The anger was general. Sadique's wife was somehow everyone's wife or mother or sister or whatever, even for people who had never known Burhan or heard Reyhana's name at all, and in that silent consensus the crowd was becoming a mob. Soon enough, the crowd began to disintegrate on its own, like angered bees, plagued by the incitements of the rumours. A clamour for Burhan's life took life in them, a hushed chant to kill. In loose groups people began jogging down, each unsure as the other, each jostling round and past the other, pushing and pulling and falling and rising, and in no time the entire Bazaar erupted in absolute chaos. The mob sped towards Reyhana's house, a good half mile away, and that was that. That was when all the rumour and anger and calls for the lynching of Burhan acquired a crucial sense of direction and what was simmering came to full boil and the crowd turned into a mob and that was that. And all this was happening while Burhan's brothers were still fighting the slappers of their mother in reckless rage. In witless and ridiculous rage.

Somebody reasoned to me that Burhan couldn't be found after all the madness on the road and WhatsApp cacophony, that Burhan would surely have known what was going on and would have escaped by now. I looked at the man and I couldn't tell whether he was relieved or disappointed when he said this.

I thought about Burhan and I thought about the police. That's when I remembered that I had forgotten my phone at the mosque once again.

Najeeb Maash

'There is something tremendously wrong about a crowd,' I said. 'Which is why I want neither you nor I to be part of it. Nor step aside and address it. Like politicians do. My Arabi teacher used to say that grammar is the most basic philosophy. And there is no grammar to a crowd, my son. A crowd is as unmoving as an exclamation mark.'

'Why are you always so controlling, lecturing,' Funny said, almost weepy, brown rice spilling out of his mouth. 'At school. At home.'

'Because at home I am your father and at school I happen to be your teacher. And maybe because I think you need some extra control,' I said.

'I am seventeen, please. One more year and I will vote in the election.'

'That doesn't matter.'

'Do you even know what is happening there?'

'That doesn't matter either. Keep the story to yourself. Nobody here wants to know the cause of the excitement at the Bazaar.'

He sat down, forced to give up his itch to run outside and join the crowd at the Bazaar. He ate his rice, glowering at me, eyes protruding out of their sockets like a doll's, as though he were chewing me, not the rice.

This is what is wrong with this village. A skirmish breaks out and the whole village comes out of their little holes, flocking to the scene like crows around a dead friend. I could hear the brawl this far out, some good five hundred metres away from the Bazaar.

I ate my lunch of rice and moringa leaves and sole fish and mango curry quietly. Aminat, my wife, sat at the door of the kitchen on a wooden stool, looking tense. Her eyes were on me, but her mind was at the Bazaar.

Funny stood up and walked up the stairs to his room, phone in hand. I could hear him open the door of his bathroom and close it. That's what he did when he got upset: he disappeared into the bathroom with the phone. In fact, it's a joke in the family that Funny's bowel movements are dependent on the internet connection on his mobile phone. I told Aminat only yesterday that perhaps one of the less talked about consequences of having the internet on phone was that it has transformed the toilet into an active crime scene.

I continued to eat my moringa leaves and sole fish. At the door, my wife looked even more tense. Behind her, crouched in the chair, my old mother regarded me with her familiar nonchalance.

'Don't worry,' I told them, 'they'—my other two sons—'aren't involved in it.'

'Of course, they aren't the type,' their mother said, with a proud, almost contemptuous flick of the hand.

'So what are you so worried about with that dead-rabbit face?'

'Would you shut your Godless mouth, please,' she retorted, 'and split a coconut for me?'

That shut me up. On a Friday noon you don't want to argue with Aminat about anything. I am a communist and I had stopped going to the mosque more than three decades ago and to this day she hasn't forgiven me for not disclosing this abominable secret to her before our marriage. Thirty years ago. It's our evergreen (or ever-red) wound. Religion mattered to her, prayers mattered, sin mattered, heaven and hell mattered as much as any physical pleasure and ailment, and she would never forgive me for hiding this vital information from her. Thirty years ago, Aminat ended up marrying a communist without knowing he was a communist and on Fridays her old wound from that old betrayal tended to return. What made my being a non-believer particularly offensive to her was that I taught Arabi at the school for a living. I remember how Aminat, embarrassed beyond belief, sat down to talk it out on the first Friday after the marriage when I had refused to go to mosque for the prayers.

She had said, 'That's a deadly combination. An Arabi teacher who doesn't believe in the Quran.'

'It's okay,' I had responded. 'Nothing deadly.'

'Aren't you afraid of God?' Her contempt for me was total. 'Aren't you afraid of death?' There was even a grain of curiosity in her eyes.

'Well,' I couldn't help but smile, 'I am not afraid of God. I am not afraid of God because I don't believe in God and I don't believe in God because God has done nothing for me. It was my mother who did everything—just as she delivered me from her own body, just as she wiped my behind as a child with bare hand or coconut husk. For God's sake, God hasn't even brushed my teeth. So why the hell should I be grateful to him or afraid of him or death? All things die and a believer rots no better than a non-believer.'

When I was young I could talk like that. Back then I used to be a hostile non-believer, so hostile that I had once entertained the dream of opening a pork shop named 'Halal Pork' right in the middle of Vaiga, at the Bazaar, just to offend all the Muslims in the vicinity. In those days I used to sum up my vision of the future as one that lived by the principle of *from each according to his halal, to each according to his haram.* But, at fifty-five, I am not the arrogant non-believer I used to be. Nor a hardcore communist. Later Aminat told me she had never seen a non-believer until she had met me. The sense of betrayal in her lingered still. On Fridays it tended to flare up and I tended to be careful. So when she told me to shut up, I shut up.

I ate quietly and then went to the kitchen and washed my plate. I was about to return and retire to the sofa with a weekly in hand when Aminat reminded me that I was supposed to split a coconut for her. I took out a coconut from the burlap sack in the corner and picked up the sickle from under the fridge. My mother told me to be careful because she wanted to drink the water inside. I split the coconut in two with a single immaculate blow, saving the water in the bigger half. I watched my wife as she watched my mother drink the coconut water. But her ears were at the Bazaar.

Aminat was trying to hear the noise of the men at the Bazaar, stooping low, with her ear set against the open window. My mother unlatched the door and looked out. Gusts of cool wind came flowing in. It felt unreal that it wasn't raining any more, even for a short while. During the hiatus, the weather appeared even bleaker.

The noise was much louder with the door open.

We looked at each other in silence. I ambled back to the dining room and returned to the kitchen.

Aminat kept looking at me, fixing me with her grim Friday look.

I told her, 'Listen, nothing happens here. They just fight and before any decisive knock, others intervene, and everybody goes back home and eats beef. That's all that happens here. In all probability, it's nothing more than a scuffle between Brazil and Argentina fans.'

Aminat looked as unconvinced as ever. 'You could have asked Funny. He seemed to know what was happening.'

That was right. I could have asked Funny but I didn't. Because I didn't care.

My mother placed the aluminium tea-pan on the stove and lit it. And then she stood at the door, looking out. I joined her there. The trees were drenched black. Murky water gushed down with all its might, carrying with it rotten leaves and plastic and garbage, and the weather continued to darken in uneasy calm. It looked ready to pour down again any moment now, more mightily than before.

I saw women returning from the Bazaar along the trail that forked on the fringes of my land, a popular short cut for women who preferred steering clear of the main road to avoid men. Women tended to show up on the trail through my property whenever there were scuffles at the Bazaar not only because the trail cut short the distance to the Bazaar but also because it led them to the edge of the abandoned stone quarry from where they could see the Bazaar below, beyond the flooded crater. This was their way of being part of the crowd without actually being there among the men. Today there were many more women than usual, splashing through the flooded trail, many many more than usual.

My mother picked up her umbrella from behind the fridge and slouched towards the trail to talk to the women.

I put half a teaspoon of tea-dust and one teaspoon of sugar in the water simmering in the teapan on the stove and waited for my mother to return safely, without slipping in the backyard, like any concerned son with a septuagenarian mother. I leant over and peered. The lower half of the kitchen wall was splattered with dirt, the papaya tree had snapped in two and its upper half was right atop the chicken coop. I could hear the hens in the coop clucking groggily at this brief reprieve from the fierce week-long rain. I could hear the cocks, agog, crowing from all over the neighbourhood as if, after an endless night, it was finally morning. The whole neighbourhood had turned into a parliament of toads.

I could see more women return to their homes, stopping to talk to the newly arriving women, some leaving halfway with them without shambling all the way up to the edge of the quarry through the crannied path. But my mother wasn't one among the returnees. So I went back and turned off the stove and placed a lid over the pan. I was about to go back to the door to wait for my mother when I heard a thudding sound, like someone jumping from the first floor and landing expertly in the wet sand. That had to be my son.

'There goes your son,' I said.

'He isn't gone anywhere,' Aminat said. 'Just don't bother him so much.'

I said nothing. I just went up into his room and opened his bathroom. He was gone. He had gone to join the crowd. I returned to the kitchen door to wait for my mother. I said nothing to Aminat.

My mother returned, shambling through the water.

'Found out?' I said. 'Had your curiosity clarified, Umma?'

'It's nothing like what you imagine. It's something else.'

'What am I imagining?'

'Some football thing you were saying, a scuffle between Brazil-Argentina fans or something.'

'Ah that.' Sure, I knew it wasn't that. It was far too raucous for that. 'So what else is it about, Umma?'

'Let me tell you.' She gasped a little as she sat down on her chair. 'Let me breathe a little.'

'Oh, breathe as much as you want, Umma,' I said. 'The air is all yours. Shall I warm some rice and scrape some coconut for you meanwhile? The tea is ready.'

'It's something involving Burhan,' she said, 'that Nabeesu's youngest, and Reyhana, that wife of Sadique, Noorjahan's son.'

'Sadique's wife? The lady whose girls are studying medicine? I taught them while they were in school. Brilliant girls.'

'Yes, that's her.'

'So what's up with them?'

'Well, they have been meeting in the nights and doing things, I suppose. I don't know.' She was breathing heavily.

'They were doing what things, Umma?'

'I am seventy-three and you are fifty-five,' she said. 'Now, tell me, need I tell you what all things a grown-up man and grown-up woman do?'

'Well,' I paused, 'well, you needn't, Umma.'

'Stupid,' Aminat muttered.

'Damn right,' her mother-in-law agreed.

'Well, that happens quite a lot here, I imagine,' I said.

'What happens quite a lot here?' My mother sounded angry. 'What do you imagine?'

'Well, every third husband in and around our village is in the Gulf.'

'So?'

'So? So what? Things happen, Umma, Things happen. The same Things you alluded to a moment ago. When every third husband in and around the village is in the Gulf, Things are bound to happen.'

'Well, when Things happen, Things are found out, because nothing rots for long in secrecy. Then there is trouble.'

'So what is the trouble here, Umma?'

'Well, sleeping with someone else's wife itself is trouble. And then he is twenty-five and she, forty or forty-five. Forty or forty-five, I said.'

'Umma, wasn't the Prophet twenty-five when he married Khadijah?'

That quieted my mother for a moment. I could hear her quiet anger. I could feel on my skin the silent stare of Aminat. They don't much like this business of dragging the Prophet's name so trivially into domestic banter.

She let a moment pass before reprimanding me. 'Burhan is not Prophet Muhammad.'

'That's right, Umma. Burhan is not Prophet Muhammad. I was just pointing out that the age-difference shouldn't be an issue. That's all. I sincerely apologise. So tell me what happened. What's all this excitement at the Bazaar about?'

'It's a bit knotty. Let me breathe a little.'

My mother took time slowing down her laborious breathing.

She has a strong heart but weak lungs. Just like me. Aminat moved her wooden stool along the wall and sat down by my mother, ready to listen to her account. I mounted the pathiri chatty on the stove and warmed some rice and scraped coconut into a steel bowl. It didn't take me more than three minutes to do all this. And then I sprinkled the coconut shreds and rice into a cup and poured black tea into it. My mother took the cup from me and placed it on the stool of the window right behind her. Then she gave us a quick synopsis of what had led to what.

'So the whole excitement is about four men defending the honour of their mother against four men who have come to avenge the dishonour to their brother and uncle, Sadique C.T. And while all this is going on, the protagonist of the circus is—guess where?—yes, in Reyhana's lap, RIGHT NOW, they say, comfortably naked, on a Friday afternoon, and both of their phones are switched off. Or so they tell me. The news has been spreading from phone to phone and, except for us, everyone in the village knows the news, it seems. Now the crowd of spectators has gone rogue. A mob has started off to beat up Burhan. Beat up or kill. I don't know. Women were saying all kinds of things. I don't know the truth of everything. All I know is that it is a fact that the crowd has gone rogue.'

The story my mother told sounded too coherent to disbelieve. I stared at her, stunned. 'And they have gone to kill Burhan, you say.'

'That's what they said.'

'How do you know all this?'

'You saw me go out. I talked to people. They also said it's all on the phone. On WhatsApp.'

'And you say they say a mob has started off to kill Burhan?'

'If they find him, they might well end up killing him,' she said. 'That's a mob of more than five hundred, they say.'

'Five hundred?' I almost yelled.

My mother didn't reply to that. She crouched in her chair and sipped her tea with the rice and coconut shreds in it. On her face that familiar nonchalance was back.

The whole story troubled me. Scared me. I went to my bedroom and turned my phone on. My first instinct was to call Funny and order him back home. Instead, I dialled 100 for the police.

Funny

Nothing weighs on my mind like the burden of my father. With him around even breathing is burdensome. Perhaps if I were brought up in my mother's faith and not in my father's faithlessness, I would have been able to witness the whole thing. From beginning to end. But my father never went to the mosque and never let my mother send me.

So I happened to be home when all this was happening and my father was home. My mind was aching with the burden of my father, always so controlling, always so patronising, always lecturing me about one virtue or another in his slow dispassionate sentences. He was sitting right there, refusing to let me go out and take a look at what was going on at the Bazaar, stopping me from speaking a single sentence about what was going on at the

Bazaar, and then lecturing me about what his Arabi teacher had to say about crowds or mobs. So I went up the stairs and went into my bathroom with my phone in my hand and watched porn to de-stress, cursing my father for being my father and cursing God for not being my God. I sank my teeth into my lower lip in frustration.

I can never forgive my father for being my father. For rearing me like a tomato plant, prone to falling and dying without external support. For pruning me like a girl, for never buying me a bicycle let alone motorcycle, for not allowing me to go to a movie on my own, for not letting me go to Kozhikode on my own like my classmates and friends in the village do, to spend time on the beach and check into the malls and check out girls shopping at Sweet Meat Street and stroll around town in purposeless, fatherless freedom. I can never forgive my father for never once allowing me to go up the hill or down to the river. I can never forgive my father for never teaching me nor giving me a chance to learn how to swim. For rearing me like some exam-plant something, the sole responsibility of which was to keep on giving seasonal fruits in the form of better examination results. All the time better. I can never forgive my father for denying me each little adventure of boyhood with that gummy adhesive insular emotion he calls Love.

In our house even getting a hundred rupees from my father involved an elaborate procedure. The application had to go through my mother before he called me for an interview to verify the justifiability of my claim to a hundred rupees. Even while allowing me to use the new phone—an Apple iPhone SE that my cousin had brought for me as a gift all the way from Dubai two months ago—there were gruelling interviews and cruel terms and conditions. I could use the phone today because it was a holiday and it was a holiday because the District Collector had declared the day a holiday owing to the deluge. On non-holidays I could only use my phone for an hour in the morning and an hour in the evening, eight to nine and six to seven respectively.

My mental health was smarting under the constant shadow of his soldierly vigilance. I mean the world to him and I don't know what he will do without me. But I know what I will do without him: I will do everything he never lets me do. For example, every single boy from the village except Arun and I was out at the Bazaar—even boys far younger than us. Arun, my friend and classmate, also has a martinet for a father (ex-military at that) although he doesn't hate his father as much as I hate mine. They were all out watching the fight, updating the whole thing live on WhatsApp. Even the women were out, watching. It frustrated me beyond words. I could have been one among them, witnessing all the madness at the Bazaar. Instead, I had to shut myself inside a dim bathroom and be content with watching the peeks and glances offered by the videos forwarded on WhatsApp.

So I bit my lower lip and cursed my father. Watching porn. Watching *Japanese Mature Woman Lactating into Not-Husband's Mouth* at *nipponcreampie.com.* Because watching porn was what I did whenever I had to give vent to my frustration. Watching porn had always been a thoroughly de-stressing exercise for me. Usually, that is. But not today. I tried to ignore WhatsApp for a moment and concentrate on the porn. I closed one incognito window and opened another and played *BoobyRussianMother-in-lawCan'tResistNaked-sleepingSon-in-law'sCock* at *matureboobies.com.* I liked porn with a story to tell. And today there was some real context after all. The sleeping teenage-looking son-in-law lay naked in his bed in teenage innocence, his penis sinfully erect somehow under the thin nylon sheet he had covered himself with till his hips, and the fiftyish-looking mother-in-law stood by him in the dim light of the table lamp, staring at him, consumed by a lust that her eyes and hands couldn't contain. She untied the floral babushka from under her chin and swivelled her neck, dishevelling her long straight Rapunzel locks, and took a couple of nervous steps closer to the bed, flipping the light bulb on, her restless hands stroking her thighs, her lips muttering something in Russian. I yearned for subtitles. She took off her sleeveless burgundy nightie unravelling her luscious anatomy and unhooked the push-up bra and dropped the satin thongs to her ankles, also losing the blonde merkin that adorned her mons along with it, and for a moment I was intrigued even though I had watched the video a dozen times, so anxious about her next move that I bit my nail as if I had no idea what was going to happen next.

Arun phoned, interrupting the video. This was Arun's way of releasing his own frustration: by phoning me. I was in no mood but I answered the call anyway.

'I am right here,' he said. 'Look out of the window.'

'Where?'

'Right below. Look out of the window.'

'Okay.' I came out of my bathroom and looked out of the window. Arun stood there, waving the hand with the phone my way. 'What's up?'

'Come down.'

I looked at him suspiciously. Not understanding what he was suggesting. 'Ippa is home.'

'Jump,' he hissed.

I looked at him in a kind of incredulous surmise.

'Okay,' I said. 'Stay where you are. Let me try.'

I opened my door and slunk out on my toes to the balcony and jumped into the wet sand below, adventuring my way out to freedom. In my hurry I left Arun behind and had to wait for him. We took the shortcut around the cashew plantation and emerged at the drop of the quarry. People were deserting the Bazaar in droves, breaking away from the ring around the fighters, towards the fields, and they looked far more than five hundred in strength—almost a thousand. I had never seen anything like it before. There was a sense of fatal attraction in the sight, an aura of urgency that drove you to be part of it with a kick on the butt. With a blow on the back of your head. They looked like wildebeests during great migrations on the African veldts and this was more exciting and scarier than what my father had warned. I had never seen a greater spectacle than a mob on the move. It had a highly infectious appeal, a sudden burgeoning of fear that couldn't hold you back from becoming part of it. You wanted to become part of it because others were becoming part of it because that's how a mob is made possible. And that's exactly how it looked from this far up, that's how looking at it made me feel. Our phones were twittering like birds with WhatsApp alerts. We both clicked pictures of the scene for a few seconds and sent them to friends instantly. Then we skidded down the rock and waded across the logged water a good half circle round the quarry, entering the main road and joining the mob at its head. It was all very exciting and scary. A kind of sustained and unabsorbable shock, a feeling that made me feel wanted, feel afraid of myself. It all looked too manly for me, too much heart and lungs and hot blood. Like the body was no longer within the mind's control and I ran like mad, like all the others, surrendering to the throbbing urgency of it all, and I was the mob.

Deepu

The whole afternoon was extraordinarily eventful. Ridiculously dramatic. Too real and too bloody to disbelieve.

I was as enraged as the others when I heard that Burhan was back in Reyhana's house. Extramarital affairs were not something we expected to be in vogue here. And here, unlike in the other instances, it was even more grotesque because Reyhana was as old as my mother, with children who were as old as me, and I was only two years younger than Burhan. The news violated something profound in me, something I couldn't name.

Of course, this wasn't the first extramarital affair in the village. But, whenever you heard about it, you heard about it later, when the affair had already reached its climax in a successful elopement, or afterwards, when the whole thing had been hushed up and all that was left were crumbs of salacious gossip. It had happened with Shahid as well, some couple years ago, when he was still in the Gulf (Saudi Arabia, I think), when his then wife, too beautiful for him by general agreement and too voluptuous to be satisfied by his female dick, ran away with a madrassa teacher from Gudalur who, aside from being darker, was not better looking than Shahid at all. She ran away with the madrassa guy a day before Shahid was scheduled to return home. After finding out that his wife had left—she sent him a message with three of those waving-hand emojis on WhatsApp, people said—the poor guy had to postpone his homecoming by a full year due to the sheer humiliation his wife had brought upon him by deserting him for a man whom he called the Dark Mullah. In fact, Chinnan chose Shahid to confide his secret about Burhan and Reyhana because Chinnan knew that it would hurt him personally. And so it did. But then, we all shared the sentiment. There was a spurt in the number of extramarital affairs here, there were discussions on that in the village and we had all resolved to put an end to these. That was a week ago.

The storm had ceased a few minutes ago but, even before that, we had only been talking, Gopu and me, instead of studying, as we had resolved to. But now we were helplessly distracted.

I said, 'They have made a target out of Gulf Malayalis, don't you think? This happened to Ubaid when his wife went on a tour to Ooty with someone from Manjeri and never returned. Basit's wife eloped with a Bengali—a Bengali for God's sake—after they met during the construction of the little house Basit was building for her with all the money he was earning in the Gulf shepherding 300-plus sheep in the deep desert, and she took away their only daughter, too. With a Bengali construction worker. All the way to Bengal. Talk of audacity.'

'With an uncircumcised dick, Basit said.' Gopu's eyes were on his phone.'And Shahid's wife too.'

'But the child isn't Shahid's, I would say, because that child's face owes Shahid nothing at all. He didn't go after the child because he knew the child wasn't his.'

'Whatever,' I shrugged. 'But the fact is she left him to be with someone else. And Venu's wife ditched him for that newspaper boy, that gaunt little brat four years her junior. The stories seem endless.'

'Burhan's no gaunt thing. He is as big as any of his brothers. But this is an extreme case of lust, I must agree. Twenty or twenty-five years her junior, they say.'

'Is that so?' I said. 'I thought she was forty or forty-five, or that's what I read. I myself have never seen her. I have only seen Sadique. And his daughters.'

'But you can't blame him, I would say,' he said. 'She has such a fine, curvy, booby shape despite the age, I'd say,' and he looked up from the phone, 'that if I got a chance, I myself would screw her from her very south. Kanyakumari, to be precise.'

'I can imagine. If she can mother two like Shaza and Shazia, I suppose she has the shape because they don't look like their father at all. But twenty-five years older than Burhan? That sounds like an exaggeration, I would say.'

'Have you seen her?' Gopu leered, looking up from his phone again and getting up from his sedan chair enthusiastically, trotting across the veranda, eager to show me her photograph. 'That's one voluptuous piece of flesh, don't you think?' He zoomed in on a photo of hers from one of the myriad WhatsApp groups.

'A bit chubby, but honestly she doesn't look older than forty-five to me,' I said, pushing the phone away. 'In fact, she looks less old: forty, I would say.'

He went and sprawled back on his chair as before. His phone kept vibrating in his hand with each WhatsApp alert. Like always. Poor Gopu. Facebooking or WhatsApping eternally, neither here nor elsewhere, or here and everywhere else at the same time. Always connected to his Bluetooth earphones, always speaking louder than he needed to. Glued to the phone.

'Maybe,' he said. 'Who cares. She always looked pretty capable of raising such troubles though, I would say. It's in her very gait—you know the sight when she walks down the street, half-wrapped in her gaudy saris, choosing to leave her body bare where the curves deepen, always left me on the edge of provocation. Like the provocation of a lady at the onset of menopause. I don't know how to express it in words. She has a certain quality, comparable only to those buxom aunties found in the soft-porn movies of the nineties, you know what I mean, a noble frustrated widow type. With those blazing hypnotic eyes, like those of Shakeela.' He looked up briefly from his phone, his face vividly conveying just how inadequate words were to express the provocation of Reyhana's gait—something that I myself had never been able to witness and appreciate despite having lived in the village for about as long as he had. 'Maybe she has always been the type. Who knows.'

I picked up my phone and eased into my own chair. On WhatsApp people were raising a riot. Rightly so. This thing had become a trend—of isolating the wives of Gulf Malayalis as potential targets. On WhatsApp there was a stampede of messages and I read some and forwarded some without comment. I didn't enter any conversation with anyone although people were online, chatting and inciting each other's tempers, in family groups as well as in friends' and villagers' groups, even party groups. The problem was that, when I used the internet, my phone heated up and the battery died prematurely. I wanted to use less internet and gulp down more news before my phone beeped its annoying beeps of *please connect your charger.* I turned off the internet and set my phone down and got up to spit out into the flooded yard.

'Not that it matters,' I said, 'but she doesn't look more than forty-five to me, not by any stretch of the imagination. A bit on the plump side for sure, Shakeela-like, as you say, but certainly not more than forty-five.'

'Well, forty-five or fifty-five, we know how old Burhan is: just as old as you and I.'

'That's right.'

I picked up my phone again. I simply couldn't resist. Messages cascaded in the moment I turned on the internet. I opened WhatsApp. *Nammude Vaiga* was one of the most popular groups in the village, with two hundred and fifty-plus members, all of them men. Everyone I knew was a member of this group, either on WhatsApp or Facebook, where its members ran up to an insane two thousand—astounding because the population of Vaiga didn't total seventeen hundred, more than half of them women. Everyone was a member. From my fourteen-year-old dyslexic cousin Jishnu to my mother's deaf great-grandfather. From the muezzin at the mosque to Sharat in Tanzania and Burhan and all his brothers, they were all members. And on *Nammude Vaiga*, there were around six hundred and seven unread messages. This was in the five minutes since I last checked. I was flabbergasted. Text and audio messages were pouring in, from places as far away as Dubai and Riyadh and Al Ain and Muscat and Doha. They were all saying more or less the same thing I was saying. In different words and varying levels of intensity. That this was a disgrace. That at least this time around there should be a public response to this. I kept scrolling down in agreement.

A wrong is a wrong and needs corrective punishment. Absolutely.

And right methods to right the wrong according to the nature of the wrong. I couldn't agree more. In fact, the nature of the wrong begs the method of its punishment.

I don't necessarily believe that all wrongs deserve a physical punishment like they say they do in Saudi Arabia, but there are wrongs that are emotional and wrongs that are unemotional in nature. Burhan's wrong falls in the former and requires nothing less than a good whacking right in the middle of the Bazaar. That useful distinction and solution summed up my own opinion on the whole issue. I couldn't help but send a Thumbs Up emoji for that one.

Think of that forty-seven-year-old bitch. I thought about the forty-seven-year-old bitch. I still didn't think she was more than forty.

He has been negotiating this slippery surface far too well for far too long. Six months? A year? Too long a foolery to deserve forgiveness. Catch the motherfucker and deny him the very thing he has been fooling us with. Too literary for me, too intense.

Stone that son of a bitch. Too dramatic. Too Biblical. Too Muslim.

Someone sent a screenshot from Google Images. *'All right, but let the one who has never sinned throw the first stone.' Then he stooped down again and wrote in the dust—Gospel of John.* Going by that standard, there would be no punishment at all, I thought. And, after all, Yeshu himself didn't cast the stone.

'Wasn't that profoundly funny?' I said, looking up from phone.

'What?' Gopu said without looking up from the phone.

'That Yeshu himself didn't cast the stone at the adulteress? According to the *Book of Deuteronomy* he was supposed to.'

'That's why they crucified him. They crucified him because he refused to cast a stone at the adulteress. They did it in response to the painful realisation that the messiah himself might be a sinner.'

'Bullshit,' I said, and continued to scroll *Nammude Vaiga,* where hundreds of messages were cascading in each minute, the tone increasingly vile and virulent and scurrilous and obscene and reprehensible even for me.

It was an infectiously violent experience to scroll through those WhatsApp groups, all so amuck with feverish opinions and equally feverish counter-opinions. There were moderates and extremists, extreme moderates and moderate extremists, bullies and thinkers, casteist grandfathers and conservative communists, those who typed in Malayalam and those who typed Malayalam in Roman letters and those who were emoji experts, toddy tappers and doctors, drumbeaters and silent folks who only forwarded whatever came their way with indifference, like me, there were Muslims and Christians and Hindus, all variety of men were actively present there in that silent but deafening cacophony of the virtual world, like a stadium full of quarrelling judges who seemed to agree on the wrongness of the wrong but not necessarily on the nature of punishment. The majority opinion tilted towards my own: Burhan deserved two good whacks and Reyhana the shaming she must surely have known she would earn one day. I scrolled down, quick-reading, quick-agreeing and disagreeing, surfing through this stampede of messages.

And then there were videos, the same videos forwarded again and again, and then a different video, showing the same event from a different angle, and then a different one, in small fifteen to thirty-second-long clips, some vague and some blurry and unsteady and some not close enough. I slipped from one video to another for a few minutes. And then the tone of the messages changed. The moderates became a little more moderate and the extremists became a little more extreme. The silent clamour became too loud to bear even on WhatsApp. There was a collective spike in temperature. A high tide of fever. What was an isolated opinion earlier now turned general . *Kill* was the word.

Every male from in and around the village was at the Bazaar, except Gopu and I, because we had decided a week ago to sit down together to crack the KPSC-LDC test due in a week. Nine a.m. to nine p.m. Combined study, we called it. Even today I was at his home by nine in the morning and we were determined not to be swayed into leaving the house, no matter the provocation. Nothing should stop us from cracking KPSC-LDC this time around. So far I had resisted but, finally, I said, 'Look, it's all turning out to be a little more compelling than we had earlier thought.'

'I can see as much as you can.'

'What are we doing here then? We are busy on the phone and not studying anyway.'

He put his phone down and picked up *CRACK KERALA LDC 2016*. 'Myrmecology is the study of ants. Russel viper is ovoviviparous. The unique ability of the cousins belonging to genus Homo, including sapiens, to bring the tips of the thumb and pinky of the same hand into contact is called Ulnar Opposition. Carl Linnaeus is called the father of taxonomy. Teejan Bai is famous for Pandavani. Navajo Code Talkers is associated with WW2. The author of *Manimekalai* is Chithalai Chathanar. Nangyar Koothu is the female version of Chakkyar Koothu. Manikarnika

Ghat is in Varanasi. Charak Puja is a festival celebrated in West Bengal. The English word "shampoo" came from the Hindi word "champo". The English word "dungaree" came from the Hindi word "dungri". "*Mens rea*" is a legal term which refers to the possession of knowledge or intention of committing a crime. The name of the mother of Mahatma Gandhi was Putlibai Gandhi. The official capital of Sri Lanka is Sri Jayawardenepura Kotte. The Kuiper belt is situated outside the orbit of Neptune. William Harvey is known as the Father of Blood Circulation.'

'Father of Blood Circulation? We ought to go. It's some bloody thing happening out there and even my blood is circulating.'

'Tell me, can you distinguish between an alpaca and llama and guanaco, can you? Or tell a manatee from a dugong? Can you?'

'There aren't going to be any picture questions,' I said.

He set *CRACK KERALA LDC 2016* aside and returned to his phone. Scrolling and typing. He said, 'Hassanikka writes, *Let's squeeze the balls of the bastard.*' And then he laughed. Ha Ha Ha.

That's how he laughed. He spoke laughter in three words. Ha Ha Ha.

'What's so laughable about that?'

'Because you know better than I do that Hassanikka screws little kids. They say he refused to have a child with his wife because he was so afraid of his own paedophilia. He screwed you.' Then he laughed his Ha Ha Ha.

'I think he deserves a good whacking,' I said, 'that's all.'

'Well, it takes two people to fuck, is what I say. Whether marital or extramarital, it takes two people to fuck. That's the universal truth. If Burhan deserves two good whacks, so does

Reyhana. You can't discriminate on the reward in a crime involving two equal partners.'

'That's for her husband to do. A man doesn't beat up women unless he is the father or the brother or the husband.'

'I would rather spank her alone than lynch him in company.'

'Lynch who? Nobody is lynching anybody.'

'Well, that's what's going to happen if each of you decides to give him a personal whacking: a lynching will happen. Remember what happened in Mukkam?' he said, referring to the incident from some years ago in which a young man was beaten to death by a mob of vigilantes for having an affair with an older woman. 'Things were hidden. Things were seen. Things were said. Things were heard. And at the end of it all they killed him. There was a sudden build-up of a mob outside her house late at night and they stoned him to slow death—a four-hour long death—as though by fucking that man she wasn't cheating only on her husband but on all the men in the village. Fifty-six out of the sixty-one convicted had no relationship with the woman or the husband in question except as fellow villagers. I am sure Freud would have burnt to ash all his theories on sexual jealousy if he were to hear that.'

'You shouldn't meddle with others' sexual emotions is what I say.'

'What emotions?'

'Sexual emotions.'

'What's that?'

'You would understand the meaning of sexual emotions if it were your wife who chose her freedom the way Reyhana has'

He said, 'I repeat: in the Mukkam case, fifty-six out of the sixty-one convicted had no relationship whatsoever with the woman in question to feel their so-called sexual emotions violated because of her betrayal of her husband. Spousal murder because of sexual infidelity isn't unheard of, Cousin. But why do you feel your sexual emotion is under assault because Reyhana is fucking Burhan? That's the question. Why do you want to kill someone for fucking someone else's wife? Plain and simple.'

'I am not going to touch him.'

'I am sure. Imran won't leave a finger on your hand to clean your hole if you dare lay a finger on any of his brothers. Seen the videos already? Seen how his brothers are taking care of their mother's slappers?'

'Is it true the guys slapped Nabeesumma? If they did, then why? Fucking why?'

'Well,' he said, 'you must know that, sitting here right beside you, I only know as much as you do: from friends and WhatsApp.'

'Are they going to lynch him?'

'At two fourteen p.m.'

'Come on.'

'The only thing you want to think of in this weather is eating hot dum-biryani with garlic pickle and mango chutney and, after that, chewing on some cruciferous salad sprinkled with lemon or vinegar while sipping on a strong ginger coffee sweetened with jaggery. And here we have folks going crazy, wanting to kill someone for fucking someone else's wife. Believe me, I have nothing to slake in me by whacking or watching Burhan being bashed up. Believe me, it's not as pleasurable as watching a video of a sheep being sheared on YouTube.'

'Tell me which side you are on?'

'I don't take sides,' he said.

'Either you are with Burhan or with the common folks.'

'I am unconcerned, I would say.'

'Well, you support Burhan because you see nothing wrong in him fucking a mother and wife twenty-five years his senior.'

'She didn't look forty, you said.'

'You like what he's up to, don't you? I am sure you even wish it were you, not Burhan, working hard under her sheet.'

'That's exactly right,' he said. 'All the bastards ranting like crazy on WhatsApp wish it were them and not Burhan sucking on her plump boobies, including you. Call it the Collective Craving for Alienated Boobs Syndrome. Tell me what else is causing this urge in you to crush his balls? What is it about him that offends you all? You and I are men and we both know that man's psyche is more perverse than what he would admit in his drunkest rant and what's happening now just proves it. I think all these men, including you, my righteous asshole, wanted to spank her bum and suck on her titties, and they didn't like it when only one of them succeeded.'

'So what are you doing sitting here with all your burning concerns, fingering your phone? They say his phone is switched off, but I think you still have the time to make a run for it to tell him and save him before people barge into Reyhana's house. Jump on to the Bullet and save Burhan from the biggest trouble of his life.'

'To tell you the truth, I am concerned, but in an irresponsible way,' he said. 'But I think, in all probability, he must have fled by now. And in any case, his brothers won't let anything so fatal to happen to him.'

'Well, on WhatsApp at least, people are up to it. They are

going to catch him while he is at it, and award him and her—and all the likes of him and her—a memory to last them for life.'

'It's all bluff and bluster on WhatsApp. Nothing more,' he said. 'A lot of blood cancels out thinking, you know. And a lot of noise drowns meaning. These are empty threats of empty violence because everyone is caught up in it and they are surprised to find themselves at the peak of a tumultuous moment. But the moment will soon exhaust itself and run out of life and pass like any other common WhatsApp madness. Imran and team will pack off the slappers of their mother in the very Willys they came in. Then maybe they will knock on Reyhana's door and give Burhan a good whacking with their own hands, if they find him at all—like, you know, what brothers do to their sister in the movies when they find out about her secret affair—and produce him before Nabeesumma, and Nabeesumma will give him a few slaps too. And that will be the end of the movie. Shubham, the end. The crowd will go back home and eat lunch and have ginger-jaggery coffee and get into bed with their wives or masturbate depending on their marital status before falling into siestas and Reyhana will be divorced and we will be back to preparing for LDC. It's all just a vesicle in your scrotum. You will have peace soon.'

'Two minutes ago you were afraid we all would end up lynching him if we were all to whack him and now you are saying his brothers won't let us touch even a hair on his head.'

'I don't know. It's all very confusing. On WhatsApp it seemed like they would, but have you seen the videos yet? The way his brothers are handling the slappers of their mother?' He got up from his chair to show me the video. The old man was slick with blood, Imran dodged a blow and threw a massive punch right under the old man's chin and the blood rose in a thin jet out of his reddened mouth into the moving gallery of spectators. 'Now I am inclined to rule out that possibility. The brothers will deal with Burhan just as they are dealing with their mother's slappers. There will be no mob-lynching of Burhan.'

I put my phone down.

At that time he didn't know. He didn't know that in minutes he would prove wrong. At that time he didn't know that in minutes the crowd would turn into a bloodthirsty mob any more than I did. He didn't know that all the WhatsApp cacophony would turn into a full-blown call for blood and that blood would indeed spill. He didn't know that all his theses and anti-theses and hypotheses would fall to the quick ambush of reality which belonged to the mob. That they would find Burhan inside Reyhana's room and lynch him brutally, that all his stupid super-masculine brothers would be able to do nothing to stop it. And that he, Gopu, would leave with me, as eager as I was, to witness the whole thing because, at the end of the day, it's hard to resist a raging mob even if you hate mobs and he didn't even know that.

Please connect your charger. My phone beeped three times on the floor where I had left it, its screen blinking in a dull red glow. Like it did every half hour. I eased myself on to the cool floor, taking the phone in my hand, and turned the internet on. The barrage of WhatsApp messages ran up to a thousand and was still on the increase, jumping rapidly, digits changing like they did on the displays at fuel stations.

Please connect your charger. I turned my phone off and lay supine on the floor.

I could sense the heaviness of the approaching rain in the

distance. It seemed half an hour away still, but contained the promise of a darker, mightier, even more calamitous spell, one that was sure to outlast the one that had just ceased. The imminence of the rain dampened the fever in my blood, the fever to go and witness the drama unfolding at the Bazaar. Besides, Gopu's house stood farther north from the mosque and all the noise was conveniently limited to the phone. We couldn't have heard what was going on at the Bazaar from his house. So I said, stretching and yawning, 'All right then, Gopu, I quit. Let's study and crack this dumb exam. Tell me who's the wife or husband of the current Lieutenant Governor of Andaman and Nicobar Islands.'

'Wait.' He sprang out of his chair in disbelief, his acne-ridden cheeks reddening like a ripe mahogany leaf, and I got up from the floor as well, to hear from him and see whatever he wanted to show. He said nothing and I said nothing and we watched. Silenced and stilled. The video showed the outbreak of a rioting mob, rushing down the slope, mad for its target, in noise in which I could barely distinguish the words of my own language. The man with the camera moved slowly, was constantly pushed around, and the video jerked violently with each push, and then the man took a leap and began to lope on the compound wall of the madrassa, I think, but without compromising the view on the camera, and the moving camera showed from that elevation the mob on the move. We watched until we could hear the reverberations of thunder we had heard two minutes ago. There the video stopped.

'Okay, that was enough excitement,' he said. 'Let's get back to studying.'

'What?'

He read out from the book, 'The skirt of a shuttlecock is made of sixteen feathers. Chaman Fault is a geological fault that runs through Pakistan and Afghanistan. O blood group is also known as the Bombay blood group. Mastectomy is associated with breast cancer. Palindrome is a word or number that reads the same backward as forward—Malayalam is an example. Kawaya Ko Nami is a Japanese toilet God. The hummingbird is the only bird that can fly backwards.' He looked up from the book. 'Do you know Cosmonaut Sergei Krikalev is known as the Last Soviet Citizen because he was in space when the USSR was dissolved? He landed on earth in newly independent Kazakhstan from where he had taken off to space when it was still part of the USSR 311 days earlier.'

'I am going.' I rolled up the sleeves of my shirt and folded my lungi and picked up the key of the Bullet. I kick-started the motorcycle.

'Da, wait for me,' Gopu said, putting his shirt on.

I revved the engine in little cold blasts until I could feel the enormous weight of Gopu behind me, then I set the wheels rolling down the trail through the rubber plantation. We rode down the switchback and passed the temple and then went round the mosque and entered the main road. Women were out in their yards, holding children close to them, huddling in small groups, talking and gazing anxiously down the main road. People were still streaming down, on bikes and foot alike, men from neighbouring villages, boys on their bicycles, and women again, flocking the roadsides, in pink and green and white shawls, watching the unusual traffic on the road, some even reluctantly walking down among the men towards the Bazaar, in strides both busy and unsure, catching up with the men they knew and passing news among themselves, with phones in hand. Water had made the road slippery, so I rode slowly and didn't stop until we came to the Bazaar, the same Bazaar we were watching the videos of, the same Bazaar where they were fighting.

It wore a deserted look now—the look of streets in the wake of a police lathi charge.

I slowed the motorcycle to a halt by the Willys with its shattered windscreen. They were still there, the men Imran and his brothers were fighting, the slappers of their mother. Holed up in their Willys. People were stopping to watch them, some even snapping photos, before proceeding down in the mob's trail towards Reyhana's house.

Gopu asked me to stop the motorcycle. He is a speed-breaker. Habitual speed-breaker. He is a python crossing the road. The slowest man in the world.

'Why?'

'Nothing. Just hold on.'

We watched the men in the Willys.

They seemed to be having an argument of sorts, father and son. Saud pushed his son out from behind the wheel and, jumping out of his own seat, lunged round the Willys and slapped his son twice, holding him by the neck of his shirt. Saud's white bearded face was slick with blood and his chest was a red mess. He seemed to be either in pain or anger. His other boys came out from the rear, one of them in underwear, all of them slick with blood, just like their old man. They looked surprised. But their father didn't loosen the grip on his boy's shirt and shouted, audibly enough, 'Why didn't you tell me he had four brothers? And where is your Burhan?'

Gopu laughed his Ha Ha Ha.

The son looked his father in the eye and retorted, 'Nothing would have happened if you hadn't pushed their mother that way.'

Saud slapped the son one more time and pushed him into the arms of his brothers and cried, 'Help your brother understand the truth.'

'I say it again, let's go after the mob before they do something irreversible to them,' one of the sons said.

'How?' Saud said, 'I am not going anywhere in my underwear. I have no strength left in me to move at all.'

'Are you all right, Vappa?' the other son said.

'What do you think?' Saud wiped the blood off his lips and eyelids and brows. He ran his hand about his broken earlobe and hair and nape and looked at his palm. Then he spat blood and licked his red lips redder. 'All right, let's go and see then.'

The roar of the approaching rain sounded like some airborne tsunami. The air hung bleak and heavy. The drenched carob tree shook gently in the wind and the other trees began to stir giving wings and sound to the coming darkness and the lightning became bluer and more frequent. An Oriental magpie-robin descended on the bonnet of the Willys and cheeped a song.

'Let's go,' I said.

'Wait.' Gopu clambered back on and we rode down towards the fields. In the rear-view mirror, I could see their Willys roll down behind us with two yellow moons for headlights, blaring its old-world horn.

Reyhana

You walk into trouble idly.

For instance, I turned my phone off after replying to Burhan's text message and walked into the bathroom idly, the hum of a ditty on my breath. I turned the light on and hitched up my nightie and lifted the lid off the bowl to sit down and pee, only to discover a tiny squirrel inside trying to scratch and climb and slip back into the water with a plonk and splash. I jumped back in surprise, watching its mousey snout protrude from the surface of the clear water in the pit of the bowl. I was seized with a feeling of sudden childish disgust and fright. I ran out of the bathroom and slammed the door shut and broke into a laugh, crying, Oh God, Oh God. And this was the story that I told him when he came in, soaked in the rain, shivering like old folks do despite all the firm muscles, squeezing himself and his open umbrella through the kitchen door I had held half-open for him. I kissed him and said, 'I think I love you.' And he said, 'You walk into trouble idly. That's how you walk into trouble.'

I couldn't help but agree. I led him up the stairs and into the bathroom and pushed him towards the bowl, asking him to look into it.

'Look at the trouble I walked into idly,' I said.

'Is that a snake?'

'You are dumber than a stone.'

'Which is still better than Sadique.'

'That's a squirrel for God's sake.'

'And I am sure you yelled and nearly lost your breath on

discovering it,' he said, grinning, 'just like you yelled two weeks ago having discovered the dead lizard on the tap.'

'I have a way of bumping into things.'

'Sure you do,' he said, in that voice of double-meaning, of saying one thing while meaning quite another.

'Very funny.'

I could hear the squirrel in the bowl, the tiny creature desperate to climb up the slippery ceramic hole. But Burhan was looking at my face, with a riddle of a smile on his lips.

'What? You look ridiculous with that smile. Please. Get that thing out of the bowl. It's making me nervous.'

'It's making you nervous?'

'Very much.'

'A lot of things are making you nervous.'

'That's damn right. But, for now, you can relieve me of one by just clearing the bowl of that damned little cute furry drowning thing. And stop giving me that smile.'

'Is my smile also making you nervous?'

'Very much.'

'Am I making you nervous?'

'Not as much as that striped mouse inside that bowl.'

'I would need to go out for that.'

'Go out for what?' I said. 'And in any case, you aren't going out.'

'To get a stick or something. We need to take that critter out of the bowl.'

'I wouldn't have let you anywhere near my house during the day if it wasn't raining,' I said. 'So forget going out.'

'Then you will have to go down.'

'What for?' I said. 'You aren't going to kill it, are you?'

'You are going down and getting me a long stick or plank or whatever—or I am going to. The choice is yours now, but will be mine a minute later.'

'I will do it,' I said, returning the private smile that had still not left his lips. 'Now could you please shed that cryptic smile of yours, whatever that means, please? Honestly, it looks ridiculous. Also, please change your clothes in the meantime? You are dripping like a tree.'

I went down the stairs and picked up his umbrella. I opened the door and stepped out into the flooded yard, struggling against the wind, hitching my nightie up till my knees. I lurched towards the woodshed and pulled out one thin long stick of areca palm trunk and returned, closing the door behind me. I spun the umbrella in the pit of my palm and sent it flying across the kitchen with a twirl, landing it on its handle. I went up the stairs, stick in hand, and he was there, in a navy blue shirt and a white mundu with a navy blue border, both of which belonged to Sadique.

'You need a change of clothes too,' he said. 'Look at you.'

'I do,' I said. He was rolling up the sleeves and I couldn't help but remark, 'I never thought that shirt was so beautiful.'

'You are obsessed with my looks,' he said, and it seemed like a genuine complaint.

'Of course I am.' I handed over the wet stick, went over and pulled one of the cupboards open, took off my nightie, pulled out another, and wore it. 'What do you think? Why else would I dare to smuggle you into my bedroom, taking such a deadly risk?'

He liked that, smiled. His smile vanished. He struck a pose meek and sentimental, reddening the tip of his nose, shoulders lowering with the burden of sentimentality, tilting a little to the right, evoking the sorrow of a parting lover—what I thought was an exaggerated impersonation of myself when I had said goodbye a week ago, to him and our secret nights. And that's when he spoke, with a Reyhana-like voice and style of tongue. 'I have grown afraid of nights, Burhan. Somebody has always found out in the end and our story won't be any different for all I know. I already have a feeling somebody has. Even if nobody has, I can't shed the feeling that somebody has. And that's how I know we have to stop this.'

'So you chose the day over night after a week-long break?' I said.

He folded his mundu and walked into the bathroom. 'Could you believe it when the wind started blowing?'

The wind was blowing with even greater might. I followed him but stopped at the bathroom door. 'No. Absolutely not. It was unbelievable.'

He held the stick aslant, fixing one end at the ventilation window and lowering the other end into the bowl. 'Now watch your striped mouse clamber up the stick. Just don't blink.'

I didn't blink, but the striped mouse didn't clamber up the stick.

'Is it dead?'

He leant back and pulled me closer by my arm. I stopped two feet short of the bowl and, leaning on his shoulder, peered in. There was something disgusting and scary and hilarious about a squirrel trapped in a toilet. The striped mouse was still, clasping the edge of the stick, eyes open in a kind of dead contemplation.

'You think that's dead? That isn't dead, I say.'

'Let's test that out,' he said, and shook the stick a bit, but the squirrel was just as still as before, just as lifeless, dead. So he detached the other end of the stick from the ventilation window and slowly, with both hands, drew the stick out of the bowl. The squirrel was just as still as before, just as dead, but not exactly dead either, clinging on to the edge of the stick, toad-like, stunned beyond response.

'Look, it isn't dead, it's breathing, its eyes are blinking,' I said.

He walked backwards like crabs do, and I with him, out of the door, holding the stick at length, careful not to shake and upset the balance of the striped mouse. But, suddenly, the striped mouse scrambled along the stick and up Burhan's arm and over my shoulder and head and cruised down my other arm and I screamed, tickled and disgusted, while Burhan sprang away from my grip backwards and we both fell to the floor, laughing. Oh God, I was laughing, struggling to breathe, even as I got up and jiggled my way over Burhan and staggered on to the bed and collapsed on my stomach, clutching the pillows. I wasn't finished laughing and crying at the fun of it all, the sheer ridiculousness of it all even as I felt his weight lowering on my back, even as he turned me on my back, holding my arms spread-eagled against the bed, bringing close his exquisitely bearded face to kiss my lips made salty by my tears of laughter. And then we kissed for what seemed like a long time even though it was only for a short while. By the time we had separated from each other, both of us were naked, and then we lay on our backs on the bed, gazing at the ceiling, holding hands and rubbing feet, my mind free of thoughts.

The rain stopped.

We both looked towards the window. When we returned to

each other's eyes, he began to tell me of that distant afternoon eight monsoons ago when he had taken Tresya all the way up that slippery hill, sometimes carrying her on his back—or so he said and I could certainly believe—to show her God's view of the valley with its slithering snake of a river and a town with buildings like matchbox structures and waves and waves of hills rippling away west towards the sea and east towards the Western Ghats, the romance and adventure of which he spoiled with a bite on her nipples. And I couldn't help but crawl on top of him, listening, thinking about my own life eight years ago, remembering that I was already a mother to two healthy teens who were already as tall as me and only three years younger than him. Remembering that I was too unhappy to even articulate my unhappiness to myself in my own words. I realised that I was a lot happier now than I was eight years ago, or even two months ago. As though I were temporarily young again.

I crawled out of bed and pulled an eye in the curtain to view the fields. It felt good without the rain.

Burhan was saying something from the bed.

A small green barbet flitted across the window. Four crows, perched on the fronds of an areca palm, crowed *craaa craaa craaa* monotonously and in perfect unison that you couldn't hear them apart. Without the veil of the rain, even the trees beyond the stream were hazily visible. A lorry descended the slope towards the Bazaar and rode on in the isolation of the fields, visible like an enormous toy, audible like the hum or rumour of midsummer rain in the night's quietus-quiet. I closed the crack in the curtain and walked round the bed. 'Say that again,' I said, 'I didn't hear what you just said.' I dishevelled my hair and lay down on the bed on my stomach and looked at him, chin in palm, ready to listen.

'I said I haven't heard you talk much about your daughters,' he said, 'so I was asking whether you love them or not, what's the nature of your relationship. Just curious.'

What he said was true. I hardly talked about my daughters to him. I had to think before I could answer. 'It's not a question of love,' I said. 'To me, my daughters are like the kidney inside me, a necessity without which I will die. I have to care about them. A mother is, emotionally speaking, without choice.'

'What do you mean? You don't love your daughters?'

'Love.' I sighed. 'The word doesn't matter. I have given them all that I could as expected of any mother, perhaps more. I have given them all that the emotion called love could give without necessarily loving them.'

'I knew as much.'

'What?'

'That you would give a difficult answer. You are difficult to understand. Forget all that. Let me put the question differently. Tell me, how meaningful is your marriage?'

'Why?' I said, surprised, taking my chin off my palm. 'To me it's as meaningless as a donkey's reverie in the sun. But why do you ask such serious questions?'

'Maybe because you have a serious question to handle.'

'Really?' I leant on my elbow and tied my hair and sat up, hugging my knees. 'Where there is a wall, there is a hole, as the saying goes. Come, say it. I am all ears.'

I was looking at him and it struck me as strange that we had only been meeting for two months. It seemed so much longer than that. It felt like we had been meeting for ages. But even stranger was my realisation that I had never seen him during the day after that day when he came to deliver my passport four months ago. We even called ourselves owls because we were nocturnal. Literally. Today the day was dim, dimmest perhaps in a very long time, yet even in that dim and scant and pale light, he appeared not only different but even younger. His eyes clearer, as if he had just woken up from sleep. They had the innocence of a man thinking his thoughts before words were invented. I couldn't have traced in them the slightest clue to what he was going to suggest.

'Suppose your brother-in-law,' he said, 'or one of his sons finds us out, how would you react? And how do you think they would react and how do you think I should react?'

I wasn't supposing. The way he spoke, the very look on his face told me that someone had found us out, that I didn't need to suppose anything any more. Not that Burhan wouldn't prank me, but this time there was something believable about what he said. Somehow I knew that the situation wasn't imagined but true and mine. And for some strange reason the realisation failed to shock me. Yes, this fear was only two months old but, at that moment, it seemed to me that the fear was older than Burhan. It seemed to me that this fear, this odd haunting feeling that I would one day be caught scandalously naked with a faceless man and be exposed before everyone, had preceded Burhan by at least a decade. True, for the past four months the faceless man had a beautiful face. True, too, that for the past two months, night after sweaty nights, the fear was right under my sheets, warm and human. But when I heard him speak, I had no response to offer him. It felt as if an immense bomb inside me had become damp and with it my fear. Nothing had prepared me for this déjà vu, nothing gave me a clue, neither the mood of the day nor the eyes of Burhan, yet when I heard him speak, the only thing that surprised me was my own immense lack of surprise. His eyes were still innocent, tender, but not so empty.

'Who was this?' I said. Not that it made a difference, but I just wanted to know.

'Your brother-in-law.'

'Saud?'

'Saud.'

'How do you know he knows?'

'Because he told me,' he said. 'He told me not to meet you any more. He told me the day before the rain.'

'That's a week ago.'

'Yes.'

I wondered how come Sadique didn't know it yet. I had spoken to him only a short while ago. In fact, he wasn't finished talking when I had cut his call short and if I hadn't switched off the phone after texting Burhan, he would have kept on calling me nonstop as usual. He asked about the rain, the flood, he talked about his daughters, he whimpered about the sun in Saudi Arabia, the godforsakenness of its rainlessness and treelessness, he whimpered a little more about his unfulfilled wish to father a boy, inquired after my health so that I was reminded of his kidney inside me one more excruciating time, cracked a joke about his dick and two about my tits and the call was over. There was nothing unusually disgusting or suspicious or obscene at all.

I also tried to think back to my meeting with Saud three days ago, scrolled through my memories for a speck of a clue, in gesture or words. He had come home with his mother, my mother-in-law.

She said she had just decided to drop by on her way back from the hills, where she had gone visiting some terminally ill cousin of hers, and Saud was right there, giving me all the respect he had been giving me ever since I had married his younger brother. They, Saud and Sadique, were born ten years apart, and Saud was like a father to Sadique and Sadique was, for all practical and spiritual reasons, the son he had even before his marriage. Naturally I was like Saud's daughter-in-law and he treated me like one, with a father-in-law's detached respect. I studied my memory of his face when he had stood by his mother three days ago in this very house to see whether in some subtle way his gestures or countenance betrayed any knowledge of my affair with Burhan. I zoomed into his white-bearded face in my mind's eye, but I could detect no grain of discontent there.

I sat silently, looking at Burhan, but I wasn't seeing him any more. Instead, I was seeing myself, watching TV at three in the morning three weeks ago, for example, wondering whether Sadique would divorce me in case he found us out, worrying what would become of my relationship with my daughters after the divorce, and, yes, where I would go if I had to leave, aching for clarity. My confusion had risen to the level of panic. Before my eyes was an image of me telling Burhan a week ago, sitting on this same bed, not to meet me any more. All those worries were gone from me now, like vapour in heat, as if inside me an active volcano had abruptly gone extinct, ash without plume, and all those worries struck me as sadly funny in hindsight, even stupid. Because the true tragedy was that I hadn't even got my worries right. At that time I didn't know it and only now did the realisation rumble home: the true tragedy was that he wasn't going to divorce me, just as he didn't let me die.

'And what followed?'

'Nothing.' His eyes had been empty some time ago but now they seemed invaded by thoughts. 'I wanted to talk about it the last time, but even before I could you had taken that dramatic decision to stop our meetings. I thought you had had a conversation with Saud even if you hadn't heard him mention me by my name or our brief chat. I was confused. Only today at the mosque, that too only after receiving a reply from you to my message, did it occur to me that you might not have been aware of the development at all, and I wanted to meet you.'

'And you are surprised to discover that I didn't know?' I was curious.

'Not as much as I am now to discover that you don't look surprised at all.' He attempted what seemed like a chuckle. 'I expected you to look stumped. I expected you to have a flinty stare imploding with anxiety and confusion. I expected you to panic. Instead you look like one in a post-sex stupor, you know what I mean? Thoughtless and at peace, like you say. Why aren't you surprised? Why don't you look surprised?'

'Do I baffle you?'

'You do,' he said, shaking off a thought or two, his face dotted with the desultory grains of something like concern. 'And so does that Saud.'

'He is a bit of a weird nut,' I said, 'but don't worry about him. And believe me, he baffles himself more than he baffles others.'

'I wonder why he hasn't yet passed on the news to Sadique.'

'I don't know why. He is generally very protective of his brother.'

'Did you talk to Sadique today?'

'We talk every day,' I said. 'Don't you worry about us. I repeat, where there is a wall there is a hole. That's not a principle I have always believed in, but I here can vouch for an exception because in this case there certainly is one. If Sadique's knowledge of our affair is the wall, then Sadique's ability to forgive me is a hole larger than the wall itself. If he finds out about us a dozen more times, I am sure he will forgive me every single time. He will hunt for your photographs on social media and like a sponge he will absorb the pain of imagining us naked. And he will forgive me, not because he wants to but because he has to—because he can't afford to lose me, because he doesn't have an existence except in reference to me.'

'I never understand why women are so complicated to understand. Even illiteracy doesn't seem to affect your eloquence. Sometimes you sound too much like my mother.'

'Women and complexity. You understand neither. Burhan, women are a bit more complex than boobs. You understand neither not because you are young but because you are a man and a man can't understand what it is to have the spittle of the man you hate on your breasts night after night, just as he can't understand what it is to wash the plate of the belching husband whom you hate five times a day.'

'So what will happen?' He looked either curious or concerned, I couldn't tell which.

'Well, if he finds out about us, maybe he will buy a ticket and catch a flight and descend on the house. He will cry for a long while, I imagine. He will add this instance to the long list of sacrifices he has made. Then I will cram my right boob into his swarthy noisome mouth because that's what he will expect me to and I will do so dutifully, absorbing the frothy disgust of it all. That's what I imagine will happen. And all the trouble will pass like a soundless fart.'

'You could be less graphic and metaphoric.'

'And he is going to find out soon anyway because any road the news has taken to reach Saud is just as capable of finding Sadique's ears too.'

'Tell me how we can come through the situation,' he said. 'Simply. Understandably. The best thing to do now is not to do anything at all. The best thing to do now is not to meet any more. Let's not ignite this like any random spark, is what I say.'

'How upset was he?' I asked.

'Saud? He sounded aggressive but he didn't look aggressive, even when he said he'd chop me up into pieces if I entered your premises one more time.' He snickered. 'But what is he like? I mean, what is his nature like?'

'He drinks tea as thick as rum. He considers himself father to Sadique, not brother. He isn't very intelligent even though his reserved nature might betray the exact opposite impression. I tend to think that he's just a confused old fellow, but then he's a man and men are full of deadly egos. My mother used to say that men don't live as long as women because of their egos. They live by their ego and die by it. They are consumed by it like a wick by fire. So I can't tell you what his nature is like. Who knows, he might hold himself responsible for my extramarital adventure because he considers himself father to my husband, not brother. And a woman in a family is a wife to all.'

He wasn't listening to me. His countenance had changed. I have walked into trouble idly, he seemed to be telling himself, and he seemed to be cursing himself for it.

Of course. The matter was serious. Few things are more real on earth than disgrace, and gossip is vicious here. It has the power to change the course of your life. The dishonour could be so devastating that it could uproot a family from their ancestral village and transport them to some distant place where they don't know them and their dappled sexual history So, for a young man like him, too much was at stake if the affair became news in the village. No respectable family would offer him a wife, and even his brothers' prospects would suffer because of the disrepute. Even my own status would be no less than that of a whore. But I was futureless before I met him and already into my menopausal forties, with a second-hand kidney at that. So, for all practical reasons, I had no future to lose by the loss of my reputation, only continuity with the black-and-white past he had interrupted for a brief but colourful two months. Not that it didn't matter. Infamy would surely follow me to my grave, I knew, and I was indeed on the verge of becoming the bitch from those village legends I had nightmares about, I was on the verge of exposing my daughters to the worst kind of public embarrassment.

The thoughts of the possible consequences of his revelation began to bother me a little but not enough to strain or stress the startling calm of my mind. Even my otherwise palpitant heart beat less laboriously, untroubled. I can't explain why but, deep inside, I might as well have been pleased with how things were transpiring and how things might transpire between Sadique and me. This egg on his face was long overdue, the consequences be damned.

'Who do you reckon took the news to Saud? Do you have any idea who might have seen you or known about us?'

'How do I know?' He was silent for a few seconds, his

eyes pensive. 'Rafeed, one of the two guys at the travel agency, remember?'

I recognised his name but couldn't remember his face. 'What of him?'

'Well,' he sighed, 'well, Rafeed and I had a quarrel over Fouziya, my cousin.' He stopped to sigh and continued. 'Rafeed is friends with Saud's son, Fawaz. I wonder if that might be the route the news took to reach Saud.'

'Maybe be. And what was that—over whom and what did you quarrel with Rafeed? I didn't get that bit.'

'Over Fouziya, my cousin. He took her to the beach, I heard from someone, and did things, you know.'

'How old is she?'

'She is twenty, old enough,' he said. 'But that doesn't matter. You don't screw your friend's sister behind his back. That's what mattered.'

Once a man, always a man, I wanted to blurt out, but I didn't. 'I see.'

'Anyway,' he said, 'Nabeesumma is going to be upset if the news reaches her, that's what I am worried about now. She will be embarrassed. I don't like my mother upset.'

'Why do you call your mother by her name?' I said, 'why not just say my Umma or Imma or whatever?'

'What do you mean?' He looked offended. 'Why do I call my mother Nabeesumma?'

I nodded.

He looked genuinely puzzled, as if he had never pondered this question and now he had to discover the reason for it. 'Well, that's what we have grown up calling her. Why, I don't know.

Maybe because my mother speaks of herself as Nabeesumma. But I do call her Imma too, often.'

'You mean your mother says "Nabeesumma" instead of "me" or "I"?'

'Often, I would say—only she isn't much of a talker.'

'Ah, I see.' I looked around, then fixed my eyes upon him without actually seeing him, feeling the breeze in my hair. And then I took in the sight of him, there in the feverous centre of my hot eyes, young and muscular and naked and hairy like some exquisite sin in human form. 'Let's forget them all. I think you know that I am not yet done with you.'

'Tell me one thing,' he said, 'how did you justify to yourself your decision to have sex with a boy fifteen years your junior?'

'Why? It's not unusual for a man to have sex with a woman fifteen years his junior. Your own father did that with your mother to deliver five six-footers like you.' I sighed or yawned, I can't remember which. 'As for your question, I was confused, of course. I strongly felt there was something incestuously wrong about having an affair with a boy only two-three years older than my own daughters. But, believe me, I didn't have a long debate with myself, because soon enough I told myself, Reyhana, after a certain age, no erectable dick is too young to fuck, and that was that.'

And that was that.

The afternoon was already eventful. It was only half an hour or so since he arrived and already there was the episode of the squirrel and the news about his encounter with Saud.

And that was that.

Burhan offered a few sweet obscenities to what I said and I returned sweeter obscenities and we kissed in familiar, suffocating embrace, and what followed was quick and hot and good. Then we were in that post-sex stupor, in thoughtless peace as he said, and all our surprised, half-troubled conversation faded away like some idle kerfuffle of the mind in the dark before sleep and we napped for an eternal five minutes. Certainly not more than ten minutes. When I woke up, our world had changed.

I was jolted awake by the mad banging on the door downstairs.

Burhan was already sitting up, with his back against the window, his clothes on, listening, more stunned than alarmed or scared. I sprang out of the bed, went scrambling for my nightie, found it and wore it, and turned to tell him to go hide in the bathroom, scared witless. But he just sat there, sucking his thumb like a baby, with the eyes of someone who had just been woken up from sleep and told that he was going to die, somehow reminded me of the eyes of the squirrel at the tip of the stick. In his hand was his phone, taking its time to turn on. But he wasn't looking at the phone. He was looking beyond the wall, beyond my shoulder, pressing his lips together, pointing with his thumb over his shoulder towards the window. I went and pulled open the curtain a sliver and scanned the brown flooded fields. I could see a frenetic mob of men on the move on the road leading to my home.

'Where are they heading?'

'Here, I suppose, because some of them are already here as you can hear.' He had the voice of someone who had not spoken for long, just as bewildered as I was about how this could have happened. 'Nabeesumma is going to be really upset.'

'Why?' I wanted to know. 'What are they here for? What have you done?'

'I am in your house. There is no other reason,' he said calmly. 'Nabeesumma is going to be really upset.'

'That can't be,' I shouted, 'that's insane.' I held my hand over my mouth in disbelief, stifling the howl in my throat.

I looked at him. They were banging on the door downstairs, I could hear men talking and shouting, screaming for Burhan and his bitch. I took two quick strides and sat by him, clinging to his arm. Like a sister to her brother. Like a mother to her son. Like a girlfriend to her boyfriend. I could hear the main door break open. I could hear the rush of men downstairs, flinging the doors to the rooms violently open and then running up the stairs, and before I could let out a scream, the door we sat looking at burst open and slammed against the wall. The men stormed in, swearing and hollering and chanting *kill kill kill*, and before I could say anything at all, a metal rod struck Burhan's skull, and before I could hear his meek, stunned cry of pain, hot burning blood from his mouth spattered on to my face and the phone in his hand flew in the air and smashed against the wall. And then I could see nothing for an instant.

They swooped down upon him like hyenas and somebody pulled me by my hair and another grabbed my breast and yet another my arm and my butt until I could no longer tell where all my body was being violated and by how many hands. They dragged me into the bathroom and pushed me into a corner and latched the door from outside. The shock was too much for words, too much for tears. I couldn't believe what was happening in my room was a consequence of what Burhan and I had done because what was happening was an exaggerated piece of fiction even by the standards of my flighty midnight paranoia. I could hear them. There was a mob in my room, another story of men and their hundred egos was in progress inside my own room, and I could hear them all beyond the door, the wild frenzy of them all, dozens and dozens of them, too many to fit in the room. And in the intense fever of it all my own chest and skin had somehow grown unbearably cold.

June

We had been playing all afternoon, Damu and I. His eyes were big and round and bulging, like the eyes of a chess or Sudoku genius. We were playing *A Girl in the Maze* on my tablet. Panchami Chechi and Imma were talking and talking and talking. From my room I couldn't hear what they were talking about in the dining room, not in complete sentences. There was a lot of WhatsApp, Burhan and Reyhana. There was a lot of police. And Nabeesumma. A lot of Nabeesumma.

'Will you pass, Damu,' I said, 'will you pass the exams, will you?'

Damu never crossed single digits, except in Malayalam and mathematics. In mathematics he always scored fifty on fifty. Damu knew more mathematics than the mathematics teacher. Damu was a mathematics genius. He was intelligent in a way we were not.

'Will you, Damu?'

Damu didn't answer. He continued playing *A Girl in the Maze*. He was better at it than I was. He was better at non-book things in general. He knew nothing about anything in the books. Save mathematics. Which he knew without the aid of books. You couldn't look at his face without looking into his eyes. His eyes weren't blue at all compared to my eyes, let alone Imma's eyes. Imma had the bluest eyes. Panchami Chechi's eyes were black, blacker than Damu's skin. Damu's skin was blacker than night.

I couldn't hear the noise any more, the noise from the Bazaar.

'Can you hear the noise from the Bazaar any more, Damu? Can you?'

'They have gone to kill Burhanikka.'

'Kill Burhanikka? How do you know, Damu, how do you know?'

'I just know,' he said, without taking his eyes off the tablet, 'we have seen him.'

'Where have you seen him, Damu? Doing what, Damu, you have seen him doing what?'

'I just know.'

'What do you know, Damu?'

'I just know. That's all.'

Panchami Chechi was now walking in the dining room, back and forth, between the walls, walking fast and talking, her raspy voice getting louder and louder before fading away. I couldn't understand what she was talking about. Not fully. All that I understood was that she was talking to the police.

'We have seen him,' Damu said. 'That's why Amma locked Achchan in his room.'

'Your Amma locked your Achchan in his room?'

'It's because of what we have seen.'

'What have you seen, Damu?'

'It's a secret and Amma wouldn't like it if I told you the

secret. Amma's locked up Achchan because he told the secret. Amma didn't like it.'

'What secret? What have you and your Achchan seen? I am old as you for any secret.' He didn't tell me the secret. 'Would you pass me the tablet now, please? You have won many times and now I would like to win a couple myself.'

Chechi and Imma went on talking for some more time. Until Imma called my name and I thought, lunch, finally. But Imma called me to tell me that she and Panchami Chechi were going out, that they would like us to keep on playing the game and not go out.

'They have gone to kill him, I know,' Damu said. 'I just know.'

'Shut up, Damu. I am not interested in your secret any more.'

'We have seen him. That's why Amma locked Achchan in his room.'

'Would you stop, Damu, please? Would you stop distracting me, please? Would you let me concentrate, please? Would you let me win one game at least, please?'

If I had opened the window and looked out, I would have seen them, Imma and Panchami Chechi. But I didn't, because it was beginning to rain again. Cold and dark and ancient. I hated it.

Imam Shahnavaz

When I entered the yard of the mosque again, the muezzin was right there, busy on his phone, stroking his beard, pacing back and forth as before, his mood lit up with his incurable schadenfreude even though the pleasure was vicarious because he was here and not there.

'They have gone to kill the boy,' I said, wheezing.

'They are killing the boy,' he corrected, gleefully.

I looked at him, wondering how he knew this. Because I was coming back from the Bazaar and this man had been here at the mosque.

'That's what it says on WhatsApp. Maybe you walked up from the Bazaar. That must take time with your sixty-three-year-old knees. WhatsApp is faster than you.'

Of course. WhatsApp. How else. It's high time the government constituted a special ministry: the Ministry for WhatsApp Affairs. There should even be a special table with a special constable behind it at each police station whose only job would be to monitor whatever is going on on WhatsApp within the station's jurisdiction, someone who can write an FIR with emojis. Looking at the glee on the muezzin's face, I wanted to omelette his balls, such was my anger. I hurried towards my room, with the muezzin shuffling right behind me. I went to the back of the mosque where my room was located and unlocked the door and stomped in. I searched for my phone, fumbling in the dark because there was no light, found it and dialled 100 right away. I went out of the room and began to talk, pacing restlessly, squishing through all the monsoon's weed and dirt.

'My name is Shahnavaz and I am the Imam of Vaiga,' I said. 'There is a mob here beating someone to death. You need to rush now or you will be late, unless you're already late, Inspector.'

He cut the call and I stopped pacing and stared at the phone. The first drop of the second spell of rain landed right on the phone screen. I scurried with the muezzin across the ablution pool towards the entrance to the central hall of the mosque even as the rain sheeted down. I closed the doors of the mosque behind me. The hall was dark. Yet I thought I could see someone on the floor.

'Who is that?'

'Who is who?' the muezzin said. 'There is no soul here save you and I.'

'Near the curtain, behind the column,' I said, pointing a finger at the fifth or sixth white column in that procession of twelve white columns that ran right through the middle of the hall towards the pulpit, dividing the men's section from the women's section. I could only vaguely make out the feet of the sleeper there. I strode down the hall. I stopped and the muezzin stopped. We were some three metres away from the sleeper. Such was the silence inside the hall that, when I spoke, my thick voice ricocheted back from the walls. 'Is that you, Ahmad?'

The man produced long snore in response and continued his sleep with a handkerchief over his face, his head resting on a rolled plastic prayer mat, one knee buckled and arms thrown wide open, pretty much dead to the world, like Yeshu on the crucifix. I took a few quick strides and kicked at his foot strongly enough to not only jolt him out of sleep but also hurt my own toe. I hissed in pain and in that anger I gave him another kick, this time on his thigh, and he jumped up, picking up the phone from the floor, puzzled.

'What?' he cried, panicking. 'What is wrong with you, Shahnavaz?' And to the muezzin, 'Has he gone nuts or what?'

'Tell you what?' I said, 'I have been meaning to say this to you for some three decades now.'

'Have you gone crazy or what?' Ahmad was puzzled still, and not angry.

'You are more useless than a barren coconut tree, more unworthy than a market bull. A farting corpse. That's what you are.' I couldn't remember such filth coming out of my mouth ever before, certainly not inside the mosque. 'Check your phone,' I shouted, pushing Ahmad by his shoulder. 'Go home. You have some news.'

Ahmad checked his phone and I continued pushing him from behind until he was annoyed and turned around with a shout and pushed me with his big hand and I stumbled backwards, almost falling.

'How many missed calls do you have there?'

He was quick to turn back, looking at the phone still, and his strides quickened towards the door. By the time he exited, he was running. Almost like a father.

The owl hooted twice and beat its wings and then went quiet. I looked up at it coldly and wondered where all the pigeons had gone. Hot white dirty feathers descended in the moist air. They smelt like bad news. They smelt of death.

I turned and looked at the muezzin. 'Can't believe I am Imam to these people.' I couldn't.

'Crazy,' he said, grimacing, and swiped on his phone.

Shahid

I had gone on calling people even after the Imam left. In fact I hadn't seen him leave at all. But, when I had finished my sixth or seventh call, he wasn't there. When I had finished my sixth or seventh call, only my parents were there, staring at me, in pity or concern or alarm or utter contempt. My father looked steamed up enough to say things about me.

He said to my mother, 'A man is half less criminal if he has a pair of boobs to suck two times a day. Don't you think?'

My mother said nothing. Her chin fell and she said nothing.

We looked at each other in mutual derision, my father and I. He began to cough, but that in no way diluted either the contempt or the derision in his eyes. He did not break the stare even as he staggered backwards and lowered himself into the chair, still coughing.

The doctor had told me not to excite my heart. He said that I had a weak heart, nothing to be afraid about, but it was advisable to take care. My heart was pounding and I had to cool my excitement. So I went into my room, away from my parents, to think and to calm myself. I was thinking, trying to reason out for myself what I had done and I was still of the opinion that it would be inexcusable even if a man were to legally marry and fuck a woman two decades older than him, let alone illegally. Because an older woman with a younger man always stinks of incest. Within marriage or outside it.

I sat in my room, thinking about Burhan who was fucking someone else's wife, a woman who had had her first fuck and mothered two children before Burhan even had a distant notion that the dick wasn't just another organ.

Even a week ago, when I told people about the affair, they all shared the sentiment: you don't sleep with somebody else's wife around here howsoever edible or fuckable or neglected she is. If you do, there is a price to pay. The price would be public humiliation and, perhaps, some communal walloping. There was a general consensus on that among sections of villagers. It certainly takes a couple of extra balls to fuck a lady almost two decades your senior and that's exactly what we wanted to deprive Burhan of: two extra balls. Burhan knew the risks of such adventures, he knew the nature of the wrong he was committing and he surely knew the consequences. Even Reyhana knew, I was sure about that. My-dick-my-pussy was not how things worked here. Certainly not if it involved a difference of two decades. If you dared to flirt your way into the bedroom of a lady beyond your own generation, then you ought to expect to return home one day with a sprained dick. Minus two extra balls. There was a general consensus on that. There was a general consensus on what we must do to him should we catch him with her: we must doom him to such infamy that he would never, ever be able to find a woman from any respectable house to marry him.

I was still struggling to harmonise my pounding heart and I was thinking, sitting by the window in my room, away from my parents, while scrolling down the hundreds of messages inundating various WhatsApp groups.

I had dropped the news in a few select groups, like *Nummude Vaiga* and *VaigaCrazies*. I had called up a few youngsters whom I had already told about the affair. But, honestly, even I was stupefied by the way the news blew up. By the time I finished calling up people, the news had gone viral on WhatsApp, irredeemably. Not that I wanted to redeem it, not at all. In fact, I had even called up a select few people with the intention of trapping Burhan and the last thing I wanted was to feel regret about how the situation had flared up. Besides, the situation had got out of hand for reasons wholly beyond my control. This had happened because Burhan's brothers began to fight with Reyhana's relatives and the congregants returning home from the mosque happened to gather at the Bazaar, right under the carob tree.

When the news of the fight began to pour in, I was confused, people on the WhatsApp groups were confused. There were stories that Burhan's mother had quarrelled with Saud and his sons and that Saud had slapped her. Ashraf and Hakimaakka were witnesses. Sitting at home, I found it difficult to sequence the events from only WhatsApp group chats and phone calls. All of it seemed to me somehow interconnected and yet independent of each other. There was a raging fight at the Bazaar and for a while everyone seemed to have forgotten Burhan. Even I forgot about Burhan. My phone rang twice more, but I rejected those calls and kept watching the WhatsApp videos of the mayhem at the Bazaar. I didn't think of Burhan again until WhatsApp thought of Burhan again and by that time the tone of the messages had changed. Nobody was responding to anybody any more. Everyone was inarticulate with ungrammatical fury.

The words RIGHT NOW seemed to have touched the very heart of the fire. Just like the lovers' almost incestuous difference in age.

Sure, I had helped ignite part of that fire, but there seemed to be other forces at work too. This was a whirlpool event, a concatenation of different currents coming together to make possible a fatherless plot, sucking everyone into its whirling, violent centre. Questions began to crowd together in my aching head. Thoughts looped around thoughts, unable to solve this many-tangled puzzle. Why would Saud and his sons knock on Nabeesumma's door in this pouring weather looking for Burhan and why would they slap her? Who informed Saud about the affair? It was not Chinnan, not because Chinnan said so but because the episode of Saud's slap seemed to have happened almost simultaneously. But the most important question was the protagonist of the drama, Burhan himself: where was he? Speculation was rife on WhatsApp that he was still with his mistress and the exhortations on various WhatsApp groups steadily ripened to a feverish call for murder. Within minutes, the crowd went mad and found Burhan where nobody expected to find him after all these loud developments and began to beat the bowels out of him.

I listened to my cardiac murmurs, striving hard to soften the excitement even as I scrambled for explanations, making and unmaking connections and speculations, and my heart kept fibrillating, each beat felt like a thud, there seemed regularity in its irregularity, jumping high and long. My fingers were restless on the phone, moving from one video to another, from one group to another, trying to believe what was happening.

It's hard to say how long I spent slumped in my chair, but it would have been at least five or ten minutes after they had started mangling Burhan that my father dashed the door to my room against the wall, interrupting the simmering silence, staring at me with his owl's eyes, accompanied by my mother, who looked frightened.

His looked livid, seething with frothy anger. I knew what he was going to ask.

'Why are you not part of the mob you had sparked off?' he snarled.

'Because I have a bad heart, because I am supposed not excite my heart,' I said, getting up from the chair and inching towards the wall.

'Of course of course.'

'What is your problem? Why are you so concerned about that bastard anyway?'

'Concerned?' He looked shocked. 'I am concerned because they are killing him,' he roared, advancing towards me, prompting my mother to step in between us and push him back. He moved my mother aside. 'You hate Burhan because Burhan is more man than you and he reminds you of the disgrace of your wife's desertion of you and you are still suffering. That's why you did this.'

I had never seen him angrier. Jets of spittle sprayed out of his mouth. His breathing grew heavier and I could see the struggle in his throat. He was louder than the rain and the rain was now louder than the pre-noon rain. On the wall, the bulb flashed brightly for a moment and then died with the click and hiss of a beetle's suicide on glass.

'I hate Burhan because I am less man than him? What does that even mean?' I shouted back.

'I mean you hate Burhan because he can do things you can't do. Don't feign you don't know what both of us know, what your mother knows, what the whole village knows.'

'What is it that Burhan can do and I can't? What does the village know?''

'You are not your child's father. That's what the village knows. Your rage is the rage of impotence. Your rage is the rage of someone whose wife had a kid with someone else and left him with its father.' His forefinger was almost touching the tip of my nose, shaking violently like the finger of someone with Boxer Ali's disease.

No, my erection has never been limp. No, I am not impotent. If impotence could be blamed for my wife eloping with that Dark Mullah, it could only be the impotence of space, the distance of thousands of miles, because, after the marriage, we had mostly lived apart, she in Kerala, in my house with my parents, and I in Saudi Arabia.

'Is Sadique also impotent? Is that why his wife is sleeping with Burhan? Who told you I am impotent? God, I can't believe you are my father,' I said.

'Well, I can't believe it either.' I thought he was responding to me, but his eyes were trained at my mother. Then he hurled his eyes back at me, spoke to me even before he saw me, 'And yes, I also can't believe that you are the father of that boy you once called son despite your claims. We know it and we have evidence.'

My nostrils flared in fury. I had never had a conversation of this kind with my father. He, by his words alone, was skinning me with a knife of salt before my own mother. I felt naked.

'I know Burhan's father. I have been friend to him for more years than you have walked on the earth.' He wiped the spittle on the corner of his lips with the heel of his hand. 'I didn't beget you to kill someone else's son.'

'I begat him,' my mother, so far silent and frightened, now retorted, 'not you.'

'Sure, you did,' he shot back, 'and maybe I had no role in it either.'

It was the second time he was saying this. I felt like slapping him.

'You damn well know the seed was yours,' my mother said, 'and I pity that even being a father for thirty-six years hasn't been able to give you some discipline of tongue if not thought.'

'There is only one connection between me and Sadique,' I said, 'and it's not impotence. It's the fact we both work abroad, in the Gulf. We live and work so far away from home to feed those at home. And it's not something that is unique to Sadique and I. There are many many wives like his and mine and yes, I do intend to put an end to this, here in this village at least, and yes, it feels personal to do this to Burhan. It feels exciting. It fucking does. Grow angrier and I don't give a damn about your anger. Especially yours. Because you were the man in the house and it was your daughter-in-law who smuggled in a man under your watch. And from the way you are going on and on, I do even have a feeling that you knew it, that you allowed it because, unlike most fathers, you don't seem to like your son very much. Well, you know what, Saud is not you. And the men in the village is not you, but me. That's why they are taking care of his adventure. And you are a liar,' I cried, because he was a liar. 'I am as much a man as anyone else. How the fuck do you know I am impotent? Did she tell you that? Did she tell you that your son is impotent?'

''Why don't you ask that your mother?'

'Shut your foul mouths and hush now,' my mother cried, 'both of you. Or I will—'

'I hate you,' I snarled at my father, 'I hate you.'

He laughed. 'It's been more than two years since your wife left you for that poor mullah and even now you aren't interested in retrieving the boy because the boy doesn't belong to you—' he looked ready to fall into another coughing fit when he broke his sentence to snatch some breath, but he continued his mad tirade, '—as she herself has confessed to us. Not once but multiple times. And whom have you chosen to avenge your rotten, two-year-old humiliation? The son of Ahmad and Nabeesumma. And do you even know who Nabeesumma is? Do you know I used to sit beside her on the baking concrete floor while she suckled her boys even as she scissored tobacco leaves and wrapped beedis in the hot sweltering summers? And here comes a day when my own son has hatched a communal rage that has ended up in the bloodletting of one of those children. I am ashamed to call you my son. I regret planting it even if the seed was mine.'

'Say of me what you will but I regret nothing, including being your son, and I don't even regret saying that to you,' I said, so that he regretted being my father one more time, so that the shame of being my father pained him even in his memory of my words. 'And you know what,' I took a step closer to him, 'count as many ancient summers and monsoons and winters you want, but I don't regret instigating this and I don't care for the consequences. But how can you say I am the one solely responsible for all this? Nothing would have happened if Saud hadn't turned up at Nabeesumma's house with his three sons, looking for Burhan. Nothing would have happened if Saud hadn't slapped Nabeesumma. Nothing would have happened if Imran hadn't confronted Saud and his sons at the Bazaar and unleashed violence leading to all the mayhem that followed. It was a plot all potent and complete in itself without me. And yet, if I have ended up instigating any of it, believe me, he damn well deserved it, and I don't regret it.'

'Nothing,' he cried, 'not a goddamned single thing would have happened if I hadn't secretly visited your mother thirty-seven years ago, you son of a bi—'

Before he could finish, my mother pushed me along the wall by my chest with her left hand and slapped him on his cheek with her right hand, reducing me to a loud silence. Reducing my reckless father to a louder silence. When my mother dropped her hand, all her silver bracelets collapsed back to her wrist in orderly but violent clangs, and I closed my eyes. When I opened my eyes, my diabetic and arthritic father was slouching towards the door, his arm stretched across my whimpering mother's shoulders, coughing.

I watched my father leave, my sick father, my livid father, my eloquently abusive father. Yet the anger I felt was neither for my father nor my wife nor for that mullah she had eloped with but Burhan. Not even for Reyhana but Burhan. As if my father was right about why I had instigated all this trouble even though I knew he was wrong. Rules are meant to be followed and people have a responsibility to conform, to strive to conform, to affirm the values that glue us together and not blow them up according to one's whims. Scandals shock and attract and reaction follows, Burhan and Reyhana ought to have known this.

The argument with my father had dampened my mood. I felt like lighting a cigarette even though I had never smoked one before. I slumped back into my chair. I waited for my mood to return to its former state of excitement. I picked up my phone again and the videos began to trickle in with the latest updates.

Funny

Is there anything more exhilarating than being part of a mob? Who can resist a mob?

I remember telling Arun before losing him in the mob that we were not going to find Burhan in the room of his mistress. He would have to be super-stoned on some lower Himalayan oil to not know about all the trouble by now and must have already escaped. But I was wrong.

I was one of the first to reach Reyhana's room, scrambling up the stairs with more than a dozen men I had never seen in my life. I was one of the first to enter the room and even I couldn't see who struck that inaugural blow with the iron rod on Burhan's head. Too many men had crammed into the room, armed with all sorts of things, and I could only see a hand with the rod rise and fall, and then came the dull metallic clunk and blood flew in the air. Nobody could hear the other and everybody was shouting at the top of their lungs. Some people dragged Reyhana into the bathroom and shut her in and I couldn't see her with all the mad hair. I swung around the corner and squeezed myself through the crowd to get closer to Burhan for a better view and to even throw a punch if I could, but somebody elbowed me and I elbowed somebody and a light blow on my balls forced me back to the corner again. I leapt on to the bed and scrambled up the window grille and turned my phone camera on, in video mode, and held my hand high up in the air. But even then I couldn't see Burhan.

Kill kill kill. Drag him out. Drag the motherfucker out. Spill the blood. Empty his bowels. Smash the balls. Slit his dick. Set fire to his kitchen. Burn his pubic garden. Drag the lover out. Please don't do this. Don't kill the boy. Call the police. Stop it already. Enough is enough. Drag him out.

Voices. Too many voices. Threats and cautions and desperate pleas. A few minutes of relentless violence. Then the mob unravelled momentarily in the centre and began to fan out towards the walls and drain through the door in a mad jostle. The huge mirror on the wall came down from between the windows and landed on the men and shattered on the floor and then Burhan was visible again—he was on his knees, in a kind of genuflection, head hanging loose, chin on chest, like someone with a broken neck. Somebody grabbed his long hair with both hands as though he were a hare, trying to pull him up to his feet, but he couldn't and had to be helped by the others and Burhan emerged from the pit of the mob like someone hung to death, some spineless mass of flesh not exactly lifeless, and in that state they carried him downstairs, but I didn't go with them. I stood on the window with the phone in hand, recording the video, recording the men who were thrashing him even as they were carrying him down the stairs and to the road to thrash him again. I kept recording until the last man was gone. Then I stepped down from the window on to the bed and stood still, rewatching the video and finally uploading it on to a few WhatsApp groups. It took me a full minute to send.

That's when I began to hear the whimper from the bathroom, a soft swishy snuffling sound. Outside the house the tumult was raging. Behind me, outside the window, I could hear the heavy wind and the heaviness of the imminent rain approaching the village of Vaiga with a catastrophic eeriness. Yet I could also hear the whimper of the woman in the bathroom and it seemed to have a strange effect on the skin beneath my hair. The thought that I was alone in the room began to fill me with lust, and even though my conscience fought against it, I experienced the stirrings of the strangest erection I had ever experienced. I was having an erection even as I was repenting the thought and I was repenting the thought of rape even as I was pondering rape.

All men have contemplated rape, I said, trying to persuade myself. But only few have actually committed it, I also said to dissuade myself.

I put my phone in my back pocket. It felt strange to think these thoughts. I stepped down from the bed and moved towards the window and looked out. The first sheet of rain fell, dimpling the flooded paddy fields. I could see all the men on the road between the fields roughing up Burhan. Then the wind lowered with an immense force and the vast water of the fields rose in waves and the downpour began and streak lightning flared in the dark atmosphere and the rain shone in a thousand glittery drops. It was deafening and I couldn't hear the mob any more. I couldn't hear Reyhana's weeping any more. And I couldn't resist any more.

So I turned and slunk towards the bathroom, light and nimble, stood outside it silently for a moment, holding my ear close to the door and trying to listen, but I could hear nothing except the rain.

I couldn't feel anything except the hormonal blast in my blood, a violent desire to squeeze and suck her pendulous boobies. I was seized with a raw need to fuck and I couldn't but unlatch and yank the bathroom door open. She was standing right beside the door, whimpering and shivering a little, her face sprayed with her lover's blood. She was surprised, I think. Even I was surprised. We stared at each other in terrible incomprehension. Her sight drained all the wild sexual throbbing out of me and the fever in my blood cooled sharply and I was shaken and rattled. She was just there, a couple of feet away, breathing heavily, in a rumpled, low-necked, floral, purple nightie, her chest full with her plump boobies, her face looking a little wild from the surprise assault of the mob, the assault that had set the course of her life on a tragic path only some ten minutes ago. She was just there, looking far more voluptuous than I had imagined her to be even in that moment of tragedy and madness, and I could have grabbed her boobs for all I wanted, but I just couldn't do it. I just couldn't. The desire was not there any more, nor the will for an assault. My whole being was paralysed by a strange blend of cowardice and tactlessness and a faint trace of something like guilt. We stood staring at each other for what seemed like a long moment, scared and surprised by each other at the same time.

Then her eyes dilated, grew distracted, confused and, whimpering still, she slid through the door and skittered away out of the room, looking back, and I let her. I let her go. I went into the bathroom and closed the door and unzipped my pants and masturbated into the bowl. I flushed and zipped up my pants and went out. She was standing at the front door of the house, looking out. I squeezed through the door without even touching her and went out into the rain, not turning back, knowing full well that she was looking at me in that same way she had looked at me when I had opened the door for her, half-determined to rape.

The mob had moved farther down and now stood in the middle of the road. I had to squint to see in the rain. There were women now, under their umbrellas, in nighties and lungis and blouses, finally out on the road, driven by pity and anxiety and curiosity. I overheard a woman say to another that Burhan was dead already. Another said they had tied him to the electric post. And that set me sprinting down the slope into the heart of the chaos, phone in hand.

Deepu

'Sod's law it's called,' I said.

Gopu, who could yawn even in the rain, now stifled one. 'What is what?'

'The thing you read in the newspaper in the morning, remember, the thing that said things will go wrong if it's in the fate of things to go wrong. Sod's law. Murphy's Law.'

'What about that?'

'Well, it seems things have gone wrong for Burhan, not something I would have reckoned.'

'I told you so while you all were busy cursing him. I told you if everybody decided to give Burhan a whack as you wanted to, a lynching would happen. You must feel sated now.'

'Well, you have changed your position. You had predicted that no lynching would happen.'

'Well, it's happening,' he said. 'They are going to kill him.'

'I can see that. They are killing him.'

That was what was happening. Not a thing I thought could happen, not a thing I had even a weak premonition of even though Gopu had suggested the possibility. Not a thing even Gopu had imagined either, I knew. You saw it with your own bare eyes and you knew that there was no going back. They were pulling off quite a spectacle.

'Never thought Shahid could pull off something this big. Rage of an impotent man, as you said.'

'There is no rage more dangerous than an impotent man's, that's what I said. Because no man's mind is so empty of peace than that of a man who can't stiffen his thing, that's why I said that.' He sounded so sad when he said this that I thought he was referring to himself. He wrung the hem of his mundu. 'But I am wrong. Look around at all these potent dicks, as if there was only one woman left on earth and Burhan had her. They look so possessed by their potency that they would even fuck a tree provided the tree was benign enough to grow a couple of boobs for them. I can't see how you can blame that poor Shahid's impotent, weepy dick for this.'

Gopu couldn't quit his eloquence and philosophy even in the shitty rain. He had to go on about it even though we hadn't yet managed to unseat ourselves from the motorcycle after we stopped by the stream, ending our short hurried drive on the mob's trail. But, eloquence apart, Gopu was right: Shahid couldn't be held responsible for this. Until I was actually out there, I had thought that the police might already have made a dramatic entry and whisked Burhan away. Until I was out there, like really there, on the road amidst the chaos of men.

Gopu's shirt collar was ceaselessly flapping in the wind. Blasts of thunder reverberated from the farthest reaches of the flooded fields while lightning lashed the world in such brilliance that the dull carnival of the mob was visible at frequent intervals as though lit up by a moon bigger and brighter than our own. We got off the motorcycle and walked towards the stream and leapt on to the handrail of the culvert. They were dragging Burhan along the road from the other side of the fields, where Reyhana's house stood. The road cut right through the middle of the fields for over three hundred metres, straight and treeless, bare except for an electric post. We stood on the handrail watching the men, hands on foreheads to shield our eyes, in clothes wet and heavy, in weather that reeked of muck and kine. Parents were escorting children away and bossy big brothers were chasing excited striplings, sticks in hand, censuring, and the unwilling boys were revolting, screaming, jumping back, like mad dogs on leashes. The traffic was snarling. New vehicles kept honking and slowing and halting.

I looked back over my shoulder in the other direction. Motorcycles lined up on both sides of the road as far as I could see. The red Willys was there, but I couldn't see the men in it. None of them had crossed us either even though the Willys had been visible in our rear-view mirror, rolling right behind us when we started off from the Bazaar. I told Gopu about it. He showed no interest and continued to watch the spectacle.

I turned and set my eyes upon the Willys again until they got out, one after the other, and shambled towards us. I jumped off the handrail and Gopu too. They lurched past us and we marched after them in a frenzy, expecting them to finish their unfinished business by joining the lynching of Burhan. A lone bearded shirtless figure in a blue poncho and blue round hat with a low brim tried to prevent an escalation of what was already an unredeemable situation, hollering at them to stop even as he shuffled backwards, but Saud and his sons moved on. Then we stopped abruptly because they stopped abruptly and there erupted a brief commotion within the general commotion, even a few skirmishes. Saud and his sons wrestled their way through the wall of men into the heart of the mob and we muscled our way right behind them. The brief commotion had to settle a little before we could lay our eyes properly on what was happening.

Contrary to everyone's expectation, Saud and his sons were trying hard to broker peace and rescue Burhan. They scrambled among the rioters, wanting to stop the violence and not knowing how, but trying to be useful somehow, and, for a moment, the rioters and Burhan's brothers and the spectators themselves were confused. But not for long. Saud and his sons were too tired even to sustain the confusion, too spent, just like Burhan's brothers, after the long bloody fight at the Bazaar without which what was happening may not have happened. The rioters rioted more fiercely and Saud and sons disappeared among the sea of men and were not seen again.

By that time they had tied Burhan to an electric post by his stomach with his own mundu and they were hitting him right and left. They were hitting him with whatever they could. It was raining heavily now, darker and darker, but even such rain could not cleanse Burhan, who was dark with blood. They had ripped his clothes off and he stood naked except for an amulet that hung from his waist down to the crotch on a loose thread. Even in the clamorous rain and the equally clamorous riot of men, the thud of their blows on Burhan was audible. And all his big brothers could nothing about it. Even Imran, who fought with all his might and heart, could do nothing about it. Yes, they kept trying to save their brother, they kept trying hard, screaming in their desperation, but to no consequence. The mob was hitting Burhan with sticks and stones and cricket bats and rods in rage that betrayed no method whatsoever. They hit him with anything at all until someone swung a coconut dehusker right at his chin and he came loose from the electric post deader than Christ. Another man snatched the dehusker and plunged it right into Burhan's belly. It was too bloody to disbelieve, yet disbelief spread a moment of heavy hush among us, and a collective gasp followed the silence in which we only heard the rain.

'They have killed him,' someone yelled. 'They have killed him.'

Hakimaakka

They killed him till he died three or four deaths, I would say.

I did my best. God knows I did my best. Too many times I tore through the hundreds of onlookers and tried to stop them from killing the boy. God knows I did my best, knows that I got my balls kicked twice in the process, knows that I myself was swatted repeatedly on my head and cheeks with a chappal and briefly choked by the crook of an arm—belonging to a boy at least four decades younger than me, yes—when I tried one last time to stop the killing. But I believe Burhan was dead a few minutes before that, I believe the boy was dead even before they tied him to the electric post, his limbs were neither functional nor in shape and his eyes bulged with that otherworldly stare of the dead. I was right behind them when they moved down the road towards the fields, shouting all the way to stop them from killing the boy,, and I could see the boy up close, being tossed around, spinelessly, and, believe me, he looked already dead. Even when they tied him to the electric post and kept hitting, it was a dead man they were hitting. And they killed him again and again till he died three or four deaths because they continued killing him even after he was deader than a corpse. Even after one of them had thrust the coconut-dehusker deep into his belly. And they weren't finished until Imran disarmed the man with the dehusker and swung the thing by its pedal, screaming crazily, hurtling and hurling the thing every which way, hurting a few and sending the mob scrambling for life. Screaming crazily, swinging the thing with a wild strength, lunging round his brother's lifeless, rain-washed, bloody body until there was no one around except his three brothers. And by that time there was nothing left to break and bleed in Burhan's body. By that time there was nothing left in him to die. And his face was so mutilated that even his mother couldn't have identified it as her son's.

I just couldn't believe that a day that had begun like a synonym to the dull previous days had ended up being the most extraordinary day in the history of this village. Never before had somebody been slain here, nor set upon by such a reckless mob as this. I couldn't stand the mob any more and I wanted to see or hear nothing more of Burhan or Reyhana, so I began to plod through the cattle-like chaos and make my way back home. But when I reached the culvert, I saw Ashraf, standing still with that regrettably gloating face of his. In my anger I wanted to confront him right away. But my son-in-law came in between, I don't know from where, and my thoughts swerved from Ashraf to my daughter's weepy phone call earlier announcing her fourth pregnancy.

I said, 'It's all very true that my daughter couldn't hatch you a boy three times, but that doesn't mean that you have the licence to keep giving her eggs till she hatches one.'

'Not, here, Papi,' he hissed, holding my arm. 'Tell me what is the truth of that rumour involving you and Ashraf, about the slap.'

'Well, what?' I said, and, thinking he was just being curious, added, 'Ashraf said he saw Saud or his sons slap Nabeesumma. I think he was lying because later he said he saw them slap her twice. Twice. That never happened. I was there with him. It is true that she went down, but I saw nothing, nothing clearly.'

'That's not good, Papi, that's not good, what Ashraf did. Look what all of this has led to.'

'But wash that foetus down. She says she can't carry and deliver and rear another baby. So boy or girl, wash it down.'

'Not here, Papi, not here, but thanks for the clarification.'

Clarification about what? 'About the rumour or the abortion?'

'People are saying things on WhatsApp, you know, and Saud wanted to know, wanted clarification,' he said.

Clarification of the rumour, I got it. But Saud? 'Why?' I wanted to know.

'His son is a pal, you see? There are lots of rumours and speculations on WhatsApp about Ashraf and his slap story and they wanted to know.' He turned around and glanced at Ashraf, who was still standing by the culvert.

'So what are they saying happened? What barbered version did they tell you?'

'That she was blocking them, you see, and Saud had tried to move her out of the way. Even Saud doesn't know how she fell down. That's the sorry truth. But that's not good Papi,' he turned his head and gazed at the Willys and his pal, then turned back to me, 'what Ashraf has done, and he dragged your name in it as witness, and that's not good either' and galumphed away before I could remind him one more time about aborting the foetus.

Ashraf couldn't have heard us for he was still standing there watching the spectacle. I had to confront him. I went up to him and cried, 'Would you be man enough now at least to admit that what you did was wrong?'

'Don't shout. Have you gone crazy? What did I do?' he hissed, coming towards me, wanting to coax and pacify.

'You lied about that slap, didn't you?' I hissed back. 'And you had the gall to advertise my name to corroborate it. Damn you.'

Ashraf was about to say something in response, but he was surprised by Saud, who squeezed in from behind and pushed him a little. He stumbled backwards on one leg and I knew our conversation was over. They came around him and curious folks formed a ring, and I found myself in its midst along with Ashraf, Saud and his sons and behind them was my son-in-law, their clarifier, their pal. Those who were on the handrail of the culvert jumped down. Saud faced Ashraf now. I was right behind Saud and couldn't see Ashraf. I moved a little to the right. Saud was as big as Ahmad. I looked at his mashed earlobe and bloody djinn-like beard. He looked too tired to lift his hand for another punch and his sons looked no better.

'Are you Ashraf?' he said.

'What is the matter?' Ashraf shuffled backwards on one leg, towards the handrail. Saud and one of his sons surged forward and hauled and tossed him down into the rushing stream below. With no further word or a backward glance, they walked back towards their Willys like in the movies even as the crowd shifted raucously to the other side of the culvert, waiting for Ashraf to emerge through the tunnel below. I went across as well and looked down. I saw Ashraf float away like someone who did not know how to swim, tossed around by the brown swirling water.

From the other side of the road came the breathless wail of a police vehicle and those watching Ashraf were now riveted again and scrambled towards the murder scene. I lurched along among them without wanting to and not knowing why, back towards the heart of their bloody morality, jostling through the jostling crowd. The arrival of the police stirred fresh chaos, a commotion reckless as when the melee had been at its feverous peak, such that the police car couldn't progress at all despite all the honking and wailing. They waited inside their Bolero, watching. Someone swatted the bonnet of the Bolero with a plank and another struck the fender with a rod twice, warping it, and yet another rammed a hefty stone into one of the headlights. The inspector yanked the front door open and jumped out, screaming, lathi in one hand and a revolver in the other. Three constables opened the backdoors and swung their own lathis frantically. The inspector stomped ahead, pointing the revolver at the crowd, and those who were near the vehicle scrambled away or jumped down into the fields and swam on their backs, scared and entertained, leaving their umbrellas afloat in the wind and the water. The constables lunged ahead, lashing their lathis in fury, shouting just as loud as their inspector.

But that wasn't enough. The police was the fresh attraction and hollering and wielding the stick at the crowd was just not enough to disperse it and the police could make no headway. The road was littered with footwear and umbrellas and stones and rods and sticks and many folks were still brandishing them, even swinging back at the police. 'Move, bastards, will you, move move,' the inspector cried, but nobody was ready to listen. Someone tried to hit the inspector with a long cane and he dodged, bending backwards and pirouetting and cocking his revolver with martial agility, and fired a shot into the raining sky, shocking and freezing the crowd for one moment, and in that moment the police crew moved ahead towards the victim, swearing at the weather and the throng in the weather.

Imran was standing still by the body of Burhan, tired and befuddled, moving his neck robotically, his chest rising and falling with the heaviness of his breathing, the coconut deshusker still dangling from his hand. As he stood there, shivering in the rain, with nothing on him save underwear, with scratches and slashes and bruises all over his huge pale body, he was a defeated man whose muscles couldn't save the life of his own brother, his face strained with disbelief and helplessness profounder than mere pain. And it was him they beat now, the police, and someone had to yell—They are his brothers, motherfuckers, they are his brothers. The other brothers who were crouching by the body rose, with Ibrahim choking and wiping rain from his eyes and blowing his nose, itself bloody. The inspector doffed his cap and the constables too. They shielded their eyes with their caps and stood glowering at the body.

The inspector cried to the brothers, 'We are taking him to the hospital and one of you ought to come with me.'

'What for? He's dead,' stammered Ibrahim, spitting blood. 'Can't you see?'

'I can, but I have to,' he said.

The crowd was back again in all its frenzy, raucous as before and jostling to make it to the front to witness the ending and Funny, Najeeb Maash's youngest boy, stumbled into the scene with his phone in hand, videoing still, standing just behind the inspector, his chin touching the inspector's shoulder. The inspector holstered his revolver and elbowed him in the stomach before spinning on his heels and then he sucker-punched him down. Funny rose to his feet and the inspector kicked at his balls and Funny's eyes popped. Funny moaned and drooled and stooped in pain, hands on knees, as if to retch, but the inspector wasn't finished. He hit at Funny's chin with the heel of his hand and Funny staggered backwards breathing asthmatically and collapsed into the crowd. The inspector squatted by the body. He rose and whispered something to one of the constables and the constable whispered to the other constables. One of the constables spoke to Imran, who dropped the dehusker and stomped around the body. He knelt down and pushed Burhan's intestines back inside the stomach and then rose. The intestines came spilling out again. I took off my mundu and gave it to him. He went down on his knees once more and pushed back with both hands the slippery bubbly delicate mass inside the stomach again and wrapped my mundu around Burhan's stomach and got up, staring at the inspector with a kind of sad anger. The inspector stared back at him with a kind of sad apology. Ibrahim began wailing again when the policemen lifted Burhan by the limbs and carried him away to the waiting Bolero and those who were on the roof of the Bolero jumped down to the road and field.

Then the police Bolero began to move and the men thronged around and chased it in a hellish din, their cameras flashing. The eyeless rain poured down in thick black ropes and thunder pounded the sky and quaked the earth and the flares of frequent lightning ran wild and reticular. The scene utterly macabre and cinematically climactic, a feverish nightmare that not even sleep could put out.

June

Damu said, 'Let's go down to the stream. We have fishline inside the hole in the wall. I need to get that, eel or no eel, before the hole is flooded.'

'The two of us?' I said, pausing the game and looking up at Damu, surprised at the suggestion.

'Amma has locked Achchan in his room. I will have to go and get it alone. The way it's raining, the hole will be flooded soon. The eel will be gone. The fishline and the hook will be gone too. It will be late by the time Amma unlocks Achchan.'

I had never been asked to join in something interesting like this before. Coming from Damu, it was doubly interesting. With

Ippa and Imma away, I happily agreed. With Damu beside me, I was sure to return home safely. I was excited even though it was raining and I hated rain. Even though lightning blazed in the sky and I was scared of lightning. But I did have a condition: 'Sure, let's go down to the stream. But only if you tell me why your Amma locked your Achchan in his room. Only if you tell me what you and your Achchan saw. Only if you tell me why they have gone to kill Burhanikka. Damu, tell me your secrets, please. I am as old as you are, we share the same bench at school.'

'We saw him go to a house across the fields. They are killing him because he went to that house,' he said.

'They are killing him for going to a house?' Damu's words startled me.

'To do the things parents do.'

'To do the things parents do? What things, Damu?'

'You will do those things after marriage.'

I understood. Vaguely. I also understood, vaguely, the true meaning of the word marriage. The word Imma always says to threaten me. She threatens me with the word when I am overeating or just being annoying. She would ask me to behave well, swearing that no one would marry me if I didn't behave well, if I ate too much.

'If you do those things, people will kill you?'

'If you do those things with someone else's wife, people will kill you.'

'I see.'

I didn't think about it further and I said nothing more. Damu said nothing more. Dying was bad. Getting killed was worse. I had seen it happen on TV. I felt bad for Burhanikka.

I fished out two umbrellas from under the bed and gave one to Damu and switched mine open. We went out through the kitchen. I latched the door from outside and went after him. The adventure of stepping out of the house was pleasing, it felt like we were playing truant from school.

Damu was a quick walker and he was walking fast and I was running with him to keep pace. We hopped fences and shuffled past the houses of neighbours and we crossed the road and took a short cut that kept us from the main road and took us down a trail through the soft wet squishy cocoa plantation that led directly to where Damu and his Achchan had placed the fishline. Damu was really fast and I was panting and snuffling already and I knew I would wake up tomorrow in the bed curled like a worm with my nostrils congested by the dirty monsoon fluid.

Nobody hates the monsoon more than June.

'I will wake up tomorrow with a runny nose, Damu,' I whined, gasping because of the speed at which we walked down the slippery trail and distracted by the sneezy itch building up inside my left nostril. 'When I wake up tomorrow morning, Imma is going to scold me with a whip on the butt before serving me her breakfast-for-the-sick: *kanjim chutta pappadum*.' Damu said nothing about my congesting nose. I sneezed.

The plantation was full of cocoa pods, yellow and red and rotting. I had to be careful not to slip on the rotting ones in the rotten rain. Beyond the plantation lay an orchard of sapota trees, and then an upward slope and then the stream, and beyond the stream the brown fields in the grey rain, photographed from time to time by the flashes of God's camera.

Damu climbed a little mound and held out his hand for me,

but I couldn't climb the grassy slope. So he stuck his umbrella in a strange way under his arm through the neck of his shirt and extended both his hands to me, leaning down. I pressed the switch on the handle of my umbrella and let it collapse on my head. Damu was leaning down from the top of the little mound in a twisted, complicated way. I stretched both my hands and Damu gripped me by my wrists firmly and pulled me up a bit. Then I could climb up all right. I pushed back my umbrella on its spokes again.

'My wrists hurt,' I said. 'Your grip hurt my wrists.'

Damu said nothing for a moment. He was looking beyond the stream and the fields, towards the road.

'Look, they are killing him,' he said a moment later, without taking his eyes off the blurry vision on the distant road.

We could only see them, not hear them. They were close enough to see but too far to hear, especially in the rain. In the rain, you can see farther than your ears can hear. I don't know if that's so when it doesn't rain. I think it must be so. I remembered what my biology teacher had said once, just before the summer vacation started. She had said that we, humans, were better at seeing than hearing or smelling.

'Do you think they would have been audible this far if it wasn't raining?'

'Who?' He looked distracted.

'The people that are killing him,' I said, squinting at the road.

'Maybe.'

I turned to look at him. He was looking at me and he looked a little frightened. 'You look frightened, Damu.'

'If I hadn't seen him and shown Achchan as he crossed the

fields, maybe they wouldn't have killed him. If Achchan hadn't called and told someone on the phone what we had seen, maybe they wouldn't have killed him. I feel bad. Not frightened.'

I looked at him carefully. He didn't look sad or bad. He just looked frightened. 'It's okay, Damu, nothing to worry so much about. Because you are just a kid even though you think you are adult enough not to reveal things to me and no policeman is going to pick you up. Police don't arrest kids. Police are for adults. Real adults.'

'But Achchan would have seen anyway because Achchan sees everything and he would have told people about it even if I hadn't shown him.'

'See,' I said, 'now you know this would have happened even without you.'

Damu looked less frightened now. Less guilty. He looked relieved, consoled. Below us the stream had merged with the water in the fields. We stood on this side of the stream, on a little mound, and Damu said we had to cross and walk on the wall for a bit to reach the hole with the hook and bait in it.

'How?' I wanted to know. 'Swim? Both this wall and that wall are under water. Or do you have a knack of seeing through the water, even in the rain?' I was afraid he did.

Lightning shocked me. With each clap of thunder a fear as old as me made my body shudder. My nostrils were flaring already. The rain was deafening.

Damu said nothing. He just unfolded his umbrella, put it inside his shirt, pulled me up on to his back even before I could say No, and shuffled down the mound towards the wall hidden by the flooded stream and then paused a moment, feeling around under the water with his foot, before walking slowly and carefully across the stream.

'What bridge was that?' I asked, clinging to his back like a toad, because I couldn't see what he had walked on.

'No bridge,' he said, still walking up the stream on the invisible wall. 'It's been here for a year now. They laid a concrete electric post across the stream last summer. Achchan helped them carry it down here and lay it. I was with him.'

Damu was always with his Achchan. He continued to carry me up the stream until the water dipped and the concrete wall was visible. I climbed down from his back and stood by him. We walked further and the mob on the road was more visible from here, closer, yet blurry still and not audible. Damu looked confused. He was staring up the stream.

'What's up, Damu? Don't tell me you can't remember the place now?' He wasn't opening his umbrella and it was raining. 'Why don't you open your umbrella, Damu?'

Damu went on staring. So I put my hand inside his shirt and pulled out his umbrella. Damu said nothing. He took his umbrella from me without turning his head, but he didn't open his umbrella and the rain was washing him in big enormous drops. Damu just stared up the stream. The trees were blocking my view. I pushed Damu a bit and now together we peered. Something was floating down. We continued to look. Something became someone. We waited. Someone became my father.

'Ippaaa,' I cried.

Ippa drifted past us. He didn't seem to be swimming but he didn't seem to be drowning either. Damu turned and ran and I ran after him on the invisible wall, splashing and screaming *Ippaaa*

Ippaaa. He disappeared for a moment, exactly where the stream spilled over the walls, and reappeared again, exactly where we had crossed the stream on that submerged electric-post bridge, seemed to look towards us, and then he disappeared again. Damu stopped abruptly and I stopped behind him. Damu waited. Ippa's head emerged, as if he was hanging on to the electric post and pushing himself up, and then disappeared and reappeared in the same position. Damu rushed across to the electric post and stooped down right where Ippa's head appeared. Damu fished out Ippa's big hands with his small hands from under the water. Ippa's head disappeared in the water again briefly as Damu walked across the stream on that thin bridge like someone long accustomed to carrying out rescues, this being just another. Damu pulled Ippa's hands just like he had pulled me up the slope of that little grassy mound a few minutes ago. Ippa's head appeared again. Damu started to pull him out and Ippa crawled up the wall of the stream like some shirt-wearing lizard. Shirt and underwear, without a mundu.

I wondered what exactly had happened to him. Of course I was glad that he hadn't drowned, but I couldn't help wonder how he could be neither swimming nor drowning, how he had travelled this far down the stream without getting hurt in any way, why he did not even have trouble breathing. Because as soon as he crawled up and sat on the wall nipple-deep in the water and coughed three-four times and blew his nose hard one time, the first thing he did was to turn back to look at me over his shoulder with the scolding eyes of a father. Then his eyes turned towards the road. I also turned and looked towards the road. When I turned again to face Ippa, he had Damu's umbrella over his head even though he was wet and was still gazing towards the road, and Damu was crossing the stream again on that electric post. I thought he was returning to carry me on his back again, but he just walked up the stream until he became a blur. He un-blurred himself a minute later, returning with an eel wound around his wrist, its head in his grip, the fishline trailing in the water.

'Fishline, Damu,' I said.

Damu collected the fishline and snapped it off the rod and shoved it in his pocket. The end with the bait and the hook remained attached to the mouth of the eel that squirmed in his firm grip, the same grip that had hurt my wrists a few minutes ago. He passed me and stopped and I understood. I jumped on his back and we crossed the stream safely as before. When I clambered down from his back, Ippa also got up. He stared at me in displeasure at my adventurous afternoon. I expected the torture of thin tamarind twigs on my butt once we got back home. Ippa held out the umbrella to Damu but Damu pushed the umbrella back.

'That's yours.'

'Yes, ours,' I said. 'Keep it. Damu can come under mine.'

Ippa took the umbrella back but Damu didn't get under mine. Ippa looked confused. He pulled me close to him and gave the umbrella in his hand back to Damu but Damu refused. So Ippa closed his umbrella and we began to move together under mine. Ippa was slow and Ippa was limping and his arm was too heavy for my shoulders.

'What happened to your leg, Ippa?' I asked. 'Why were you drowning even though you know how to swim, Ippa?'

Ippa said nothing. After a few more steps he stopped. He

looked frustrated and pale. And pained. He seemed to have realised that my shoulder couldn't possibly support him as far as the culvert. He gave me his umbrella and turned back to call Damu. I moved aside to make space for Damu and he replaced me under Ippa's umbrella. They laboured on and I trailed them, lurching in the rain and thunder and the bluer and bluer lightning that would have set fire to the world had it not been raining as it was. I trailed them half-frightened and half-musing and half-amused, drenched and shivering. Soon enough, I could hear people on the road but I didn't look up until we hit the steps where the wall sloped towards the road.

Damu was stooping and slanting with the weight of my limping father's arm around his shoulders. There were people even on the steps and I had some jostling to do with an open umbrella over my head. Only when we finally emerged on the top stair did I turn and look along the road, crammed with people, all moving every which way, as though it were a conference of drunks something. I took a few more steps and stood right in the middle of the road on the culvert, among people, looking at people, dazed and frozen, until Ippa's hand pulled me away.

Then we were moving again. Ippa and Damu and me. They were under their umbrella and I, under mine. Damu's face was darker. He looked exhausted. I wanted Ippa to stop and let him go. But he continued to lean on Damu's shoulders and we went on. We weren't even two hundred metres from the fields when the police car came crawling on the road towards the Bazaar with the blinking blue bulb on the roof and the blare of that terrible siren. Damu yelled *POLICE POLICE POLICE.* He was gasping for breath. I looked at his face and I could tell he was terrified. Damu was terrified of the police that hadn't come looking for him. You shouldn't be terrified, I wanted to tell him. I was sure the police hadn't come for him because the police don't arrest kids and I wanted to tell him that again. But, before I could even open my mouth, he scrambled away and vanished in the crowd, dropping the eel on the road. The eel squirmed and thrashed its tail until it grew still, tail on head, like a ring, as though dead, and people stopped and stooped and knelt around it. The eel thrashed its tail again and jumped and jumped until it vanished in the weeds beyond the road and people went after it, pushing and pulling and elbowing and falling. A young man crawled on his stomach in the weeds and turned on his back, crying out jubilantly, the eel in hand. An older man tried to snatch it from him and he kicked the man in the stomach, sending him tumbling backwards. The older man rose to his feet and the younger man rose, too. Another fight ensued.

'Damu Damuu Damuuu,' I cried out.

Ippa's pat on my head was neither hard nor gentle. I expected as much.

'Shut up,' he cried. 'How dare you step outside the home in this rain? That too to the stream? That too today? That too with that Kanakkan kid?'

I didn't answer him. I was too surprised to find myself there, with the rain shining like steel in the lightning. The crowd growing bigger and bigger. Darkness was falling quick like at dusk. Ippa put his hand on my shoulder and we limped on. Imma was going to spank me with a tamarind-twig but I wasn't thinking of tamarind-twigs. I was thinking of Damu. I was thinking of Burhanikka. I was thinking of the trail in front of our house.

Of old Hakimaakka coming in, wet and trembling, right behind Ippa. Imranikka and Ibrahimikka's bull-like run along the trail. Of Imma, her blue eyes bluer than the blue flame. Of Imma, her legs knee-deep in the swirling water of the yard, crying Ashraf Ashraf, like a black-and-white scene from a black-and-white movie. Of Damu coming up the stairs, holding his Amma's pinky, staring at me with frightened eyes. Of Panchami Chechi, her dark eyes behind her hawk-beak nose made darker by the weather and her disbelief in the afternoon.

Ippa stopped a moment and I stopped thinking and looked at Ippa. His face was all rain and pain and his eyes were red like the eyes of my friend Rohini who was sick with pinkeye. With his worm-like moustache, he looked a lot like Damu's father. I don't exactly know why but I thought I loved my father a little less than I did in the morning. We hobbled on. Limping. Limping. Limping.

Nabeesumma

My life is my mistake. Being born and marrying and mothering were my mistakes. Oh, how I hated this job of being a mother. Is there anything more tiring than being a mother? I was tired of being a mother. I wished I could unmother them all, I wished I could unlove them all, I wished I could unwife Ahmad and be Nabeesu once again, alone and complete. These ungrateful beards, whom I had suckled two at a time even long after their time was due for six restless years while working and cooking and sleeping under this rotten roof so they could all become as big as their father, they were my mistake. These boys who had sprung on my body like unwanted limbs, disabling me by excess, who had spouted like five heavy-jackfruit breasts on my little chest and taken root in my heart, they were my mistake, which wouldn't have happened without the marriage. Oh how I wished I could just unlove them all, but I couldn't, just as I couldn't unmother them all, just as I couldn't unmarry Ahmad. Because they were my life, this house and the six men it, the protagonists in Nabeesu's theatre, they were my fate and mistake.

My mother used to tell me that I had been getting smaller and smaller ever since I got married but I hadn't yet realised just how small until I stood looking into the mirror and discovered that I had grown smaller than my mother and my mother is very small, a tiny fertile thing that had ejected out of her five equally tiny and equally fertile girls. But I didn't think any of my four sisters had grown smaller, certainly not smaller than our mother. I could hear Imran's phone on the bed, ringing nonstop with the calls of my sisters and brothers-in-law and my nephews and nieces, violating the quiet disquiet of this house. But I just stood looking at myself in the cold mirror, unable for a moment to do anything else, until my breath fogged out the reflection of my pale and incruent face. Then I turned away so that I would not have to believe how small I had grown. Frail and grey and small. I sat down on the bed, dumbfounded by all that was happening.

It was raining again. I could hear the fury of June up on the roof, crashing like a shower of hot bullets. Like a disaster.

Once again I took Imran's phone in my hand without wanting to and watched a video on WhatsApp and was exposed to the most indelible horror of my life. Not that what had preceded that video was any less horrific. In fact the whole afternoon had been relentless and unforgiving and traumatic, with the spate of videos and messages and phone calls ever since Ibrahim and Imran had begun avenging a slap that I had never received right in the middle of the Bazaar on a rainy Friday afternoon to restore an honour I had never lost save by giving birth to them. And through the whole afternoon the phone was abuzz with this news, concerned personal messages, a cascade of audios and videos, ceaseless phone calls, and I was lost. I couldn't comprehend what was happening and everything was happening so fast and my mind was already churning in panic. I had to consciously resist the temptation to check all that was flooding Imran's phone. Because what I had already seen (my four boys in a bloody fight with Reyhana's brother-in-law and his sons) and read (that they had rounded up my son and his forty-year-old bitch in her house) were all truly horrific. Yet I took Imran's phone in my hand one last time and what I watched blew the life out of me. The video, jumpy and blurry and noisy with the rain and the jostling, trailed the mob. I could see nothing but the chaos of men, a riot of men in the riotous rain. And then the camera gained elevation and the video blurred briefly and jumped back to clarity, zoomed the focus and steadied. It showed my son, stripped of his shirt, stripped of his underwear, trussed to an electric post and being thrashed with sticks and metal rods and a cricket bat that passed from hand to hand and was swung freely with brutal strength at my boy—on his legs and arms and stomach and thighs and chest and tell me where not and by how many. The camera was steady and the video was clear even in the rain and I could see. I could see my boy's pain in pain I couldn't express in words or sounds. I saw a man ram a coconut dehusker right at my boy's chin. I closed my eyes and the phone dropped on to the bed and for a long time I didn't open my eyes. I thought all the thoughts of a woman who had seen the video of her own son being lynched by a mob. All my life seemed made for and reduced to that single moment. How does a mother who had to see her own son being tied to a post and beaten to bloody death grieve? Yet I seemed to have done well—not a single teardrop slipped out of my lids, no wail came out of my throat, no scream, and after the initial shock and the momentous silence of what seemed an infinity of time, my heart seemed to return to an uneasy calm, absorbing the shock and the terror of what I had seen. My heart seemed to return to my original pang: me. As though what had happened had happened a long time ago.

Precisely thirty monsoons ago, on a sweltering summer day, the day I was made to change homes and walk out with Ahmad, with wild jasmines and jungle geraniums in my hair for one last time, with dots of henna above my brows and at the tip of my eyelids and beneath my lower lip and on my arms and palms and feet, my head draped with a gold-laced, spangled, transparent green shawl, a poor bride for my poorer groom who occupied at least twice the space I occupied on earth. The day seemed to me as old as that. The moment seemed to me as old as that. As though what had just happened had happened thirty rains ago. It seemed to me that I was being prepared for this single moment from that distant day on and for a long time I didn't open my eyes and when I finally did, I knew that they had killed my son. Because suddenly I couldn't hate my son any more. And because I could hear the frantic knocks of the neighbours on my door, women calling *Nabeesumma Nabeesumma Nabeesumma.* I could hear Pathumma calling, *Nabeesumma Nabeesumma*, knocking a little harder than the others. I could hear my name in Panchami's masculine voice. Beside me, on the bed, Imran's phone kept ringing nonstop, ringing and vibrating. I was the mother of the boy the mob lynched for having sex with a woman fifteen years older than him and they all had come to console me, to give me company in my trauma. I got up from the bed and stood in front of the mirror one more time and then returned to the bed.

My mother told me that it was the duty of a mother to die before her own children so that the children weren't afraid to die when their time was up and she was right. A mother ought to die before her children because it aches like nothing else to lose one from your own womb. The weather was icy cold, as though inside a fridge, and yet, inside my clothes, I was burning hot, as though inside an oven, and my blood was feverish. My feet were restless. I could hear the rain all around me. All around me the house was leaking, black and oil-like, into pots and buckets and bowls and mugs and even the pressure cooker. The knocking continued on the door. I could hear Ahmad now. *Nabeesu. Nabeesu. Nabeesu.* My knees were restless. I lay down on the bed and turned the phone off.

Then I was thinking. Soon there would be mourners, the same ones who had thrashed my son dead, the same ones who had watched as they thrashed my son dead, shooting videos.

It was raining darker than it had been in the morning. The day that had begun with tarp would end with tarp, I thought. I thought I would sleep for ten minutes and then I would wake up and open the door for Ahmad and feed him his lunch and give him the money he was waiting for and ask him to go to Areekode and buy a tarp large enough to cover the front yard to shelter all the mourners to come. And I hated God more in that moment than I hated God two weeks ago when I had gone visiting my old mother carrying a sack full of husked coconuts. A lot more. I didn't want to believe in God any more and this was the reason why I didn't want to believe in God any more: to make death hopeless. Complete. And what of the infamy to come in the wake of it all? At twenty-five, Burhan could certainly have helped himself even if at forty Reyhana couldn't. And what of all the pain my son had to endure? God could certainly have helped, except that he didn't. Just like my son could have and didn't. My eyes were heavy with sleep. I gave my children everything. Except sex. Of course. I thought I should have given them that too. If only I knew that one day one of them was going to get killed for seeking it. My eyes were heavy with sleep. And Reyhana didn't have a face and the men didn't have faces. They were all faceless. Just like God. My eyes were heavy with sleep. I shut my eyes to sleep the longest sleep of my life and when I woke up a few minutes later, I felt profoundly empty, light and unburdened, a feeling not unlike the feeling I had after I had pushed him from my womb out into this world. Twenty-five monsoons ago.

Reyhana

The sad truth is that the world belongs to men. A friend of mine used to say that even the sun that rises in the east has an invisible dick and balls. I think she might just have been right about that. No fate on earth is worse than having to grow a pair of boobs, she used to joke or grieve, and I couldn't but agree in hindsight. The fate of womenfolk here was sealed on that fine morning when we woke up with a bloody seat or sheet, changing our life forever, she used to say. Ensnared in our bodies and condemned to seep the blood of our bloody inferiority.

I stood at the main door watching the commotion beyond the gate, stupefied by a plot I couldn't unravel: what had led to what for all this to happen? My mind searched for names and faces to blame, convinced that there were others who knew of our clandestine affair. I tossed around Rafeed's name in my mind, tried to give him a face from my distant memory four months ago when I had gone a few times to the travel agency, but I couldn't. But with what certainty could I blame Rafeed even if his name had a face in my memory? I had no idea what transpired between him and Burhan over a cousin I had never heard of before, Fouziya someone. Rafeed was just a name Burhan had uttered and I knew nothing to suggest that he was the one who had instigated all of this. But Burhan had slapped Rafeed over an affair with this cousin, which made me wonder whether Burhan was any different from those who murdered him. Could he have been one of those who had beaten him to death had it been some other Burhan caught sleeping with some other Reyhana? The thought stung my heart like a wasp.

My lips were salt with silent tears. Tears that were equal part pain and humiliation. I wasn't even sure what they had done to him. I supposed they had killed him. Sticks and planks from my own woodhouse were afloat in the yard. A steady stream of men and women continued to flow past on the road that had turned into a stream in the steady downpour. I was thinking many half-thoughts as I stood there, watching it all, trying to digest it all despite myself, confused and unable to act. I wanted to go out to Burhan even if I couldn't have reversed the damage they had already done to him, even if he wasn't breathing any more. Each moment I stood there, I was actively fighting off a hair-pulling impulse to go back to the bathroom and slash my wrists. But my body was frozen even as my mind sparred with itself in language too incoherent to be called thoughts and too impulsive to qualify for intentions proper until I was frightened awake by mighty thunderbolts. I turned and went up the stairs to my room.

I stood in the middle of my own room, running my eyes over it, thinking, panicking that the news would flash on television screens across Kerala and a precis of what had led to what and the pettiness of my perfidy to a perfect husband would inundate phones in dozens of versions—unless they already had. And all would be unanimous in their judgement so far as my transgression goes at least if not on the bloody outcome of it because I had transgressed despite mothering two adult daughters, despite living on my husband's kidney, and I did it with a twenty-five-year-old kid who was born the year I was married off, who appeared even younger in memory. I stood barefoot on the splinters of my broken mirror, staring at the walls freckled with Burhan's blood. The ceiling fan was going as fast as it could even though I couldn't remember turning it on for the past few days. My hand went to my neck and I wasn't even surprised to find it bare of my two gold necklaces. The room still reeked of and seemed alive with the ghosts of the mob and yet it also felt inconceivably empty.

In my mind the face of the lean boy who had opened the bathroom door for me flitted for a fleeting second, not to be retrieved again except for the eyes, grim and lustful and cold and confused. A lot was going on both inside and outside my head, visibly and invisibly, but in an eerie ghostly manner. The more I looked around, the more my heart palpitated, and slowly the pain of losing him became the trots and kicks of a stinging sense of guilt. Guilt for being the initiator of these two months of profligacy. Guilt for not being responsible enough to have sent him away the very moment I heard him speak about his encounter with Saud because that should have blown the whistle for me and a saner response on my part would have saved so much. Guilt, yes, for sacrificing the son of a mother because there is nothing in the world to compare to that loss and I thought of Nabeesumma with all my heart and the guilt was racking. I thought of my own daughters and disgrace replaced guilt.

Disgrace and guilt—the two necklaces like two nooses I would have to wear all my life—kept tormenting my thoughts. I felt calm and insane at the same time. I seemed to be sweating and running a fever even though I was shivering with cold. There was an influx of truths teeming in my mind. This wasn't a house I could live in any more. This wasn't a relationship I could cling on to any more. I had to confront these truths, the social and private consequences of what had just happened—confront, not evade. I had to reckon with the coming infamy head-on. I had to choose. Outside the wind blew spectacularly in from the west and in the rainy distances the coconut and areca palms bordering the fields swung drunkenly lashing their bulky crowns of green fronds eastwards like mythic women in a rage and my windows banged without cease.

The hair-pulling impulse was becoming a stabbing need.

If I survive, I would have to wear a burqa punched with two perfectly round perforations in the place of eyes to hide myself from the public, I thought, laughed or sobbed—I don't know, I don't remember. What I remember is that I stooped down and picked a jagged slice of my broken mirror and shambled into the bathroom and dragged the bucket to the corner and sat down on the floor and opened my veins. Thin skeins of blood rose idly from the clear bottom of the blue bucket like the melting layers of the thick mud of the discontents of my marriage on my skin and I kept staring into the red water until my vision turned blurry and my mind teetered on the edge of consciousness as on a swing at the end of the world.

When I woke up, I was in a hospital. I was half-conscious and frazzled like in those days when I used to wake up after the kidney transplantation. Outside it was raining still and it was late at night. Beside my bed were my daughters, staring at me, as if I were some extinct creature born again, as if there was nothing hilarious about my tragedy, as if they had always known what I was up to and what was in store for me and they were not surprised to find me where and how I was. As if the incident was reason enough to raise questions concerning the very truth about their own father, to whom they owed no semblance somehow, neither in the shape of their face nor in the colour of their skin.

They turned and looked at their father and I turned with them and looked at Sadique C.T., my husband. The one who wouldn't divorce me. The one who wouldn't let me die. What seemed to me in the afternoon the end of life was now just another beginning of an old marriage. Twenty-five monsoons ago.

Acknowledgements

Thanks to,

Family—my late father Khader K., Saifu, Sabeena, Siraj, Ayesha Baby and Fatima Nahrin. Ambar Sahil Chatterjee, the book's first friend and editor. Sarah Niazi, who connected me to him. Hemali Sodhi, agent. Karthika V.K. and Ajitha G.S., in whom the book is fortunate to have found its editors and publishers. Sushmita Pati, Shivani Kapoor, Khadeeja Khader, Reva Prakash, Abhilash G. Nath, Arya Thomas and all the other friends, old and new. Ram Acchaibar Chaurasiya and Riyaz Mon, closest friends till the day of their death. Anisha Lalvani, friend and guide in my publishing journey. Soheb Niazi and Nikhil Anthony Goveas, the boys on the Virus.